of
small
things

of
small
things

22 Authors & Artists

Curated & Edited by Leah Angstman

Alternating Current Press
Boulder, Colorado

Of Small Things
22 Authors and Artists
©2002–2013, 2021 Alternating Current

Alternating Current
Boulder, Colorado
alternatingcurrentarts.com

ISBN: 978-1-946580-26-9
First Collected Edition: November 2020

Table of Contents

Letter from the Editor

You'd think I wouldn't be terrible at writing these things by now, but I never do seem to get the hang of it. I hem and haw and don't know where to start. Problem is, I've told "the start" so many times that it's no longer a good place to start. So, I'll skip the recap and get right to it.

I've been at this for a good, long time, watching the evolution of the small press go from photocopied pamphlets to beautiful paperbacks to digital online journals. One of the biggest joys of all this is being a keeper of the peri-millennium flame, keeping alive those voices that might otherwise fade with a new generation of digital writers. This digest is the second of the archival chapbook collections in our Violet Ray series, a succession of anthologies chronicling the humble beginnings of a humble press that was once secretly housed in my bedroom closet.

One of the missions of Alternating Current Press is to keep alive the pre-digital words of authors from the turn of the new millennium, the post-Beat and avant-garde writers of the 1970s through early 2000s, who may have had their heydays before the Internet was a widespread thing. Though several of the writers in this anthology are still out there writing their hearts out, many of them are now gone from the scene, in one way or another.

One of the included chapbooks, in fact, is a small-press tribute to a deceased poet, and now the pages of that tribute are flecked with even more deceased poets as time passes. But their words mark an era, and it's more than just nostalgia talking—this is the voice of an epoch, a generation that still has something to say to the next generation and the next after that.

On today's journey, we start with the tribute, which will get its own introduction, wend our way through the timeless work of the late Dave Church, and end up inside one of the first chapbooks we ever published, *The Poet* by B. Z. Niditch, an instant classic look at how poetry was at the turn of the millennium.

Thanks for coming along for the ride. As always, there'd be no reason to salvage the words without readers to read them.

Everybody needs his memories.
They keep the wolf of insignificance from the door.

—Saul Bellow

Taxi Cab Poet Confessions

A Small Press Tribute
to Dave Church
1947-2008

Taxi Cab Poet Confessions: A Small-Press Tribute to Dave Church (1947-2008)

22 Authors & Artists, inc. Dave Church

Introduction by the Editor

I didn't know as much about the late Dave Church at the time of his death as I wish I knew now, having only corresponded with him briefly, and I'm certainly not the best one to write this introduction, but alas, here we are. Had I truly known how much Church detested driving a cab back when I first compiled this tribute, I no doubt would have named the collection something else. But I suppose now the title stands as much a product of time as Church's memory does. You'll see within the pages that the visual of a poetic cab driver is very much alive amongst all the other mourners collected here, as well, and if you knew Church or read his work, it's probably a commanding visual for you, too. But there was more to the man besides his taxi and more to the poet than just a stubborn pain in the ass.

If you are new to Church's work here, then I'll tell you a little bit about what I remember, although the writers in this tribute will tell it far better than I can, including an intimate eulogy from Church's son that will get you closer to the man than I could ever get you. But Church's poems were a staple of his time, and he was part of a tightknit community of active poets who read, shared in, and collaborated in his work.

His death was a blow to the scene in which he'd been active for forty years, having given his first poetry reading back in 1975. A Rhode Island writer who drove the aforementioned cab—a profession he didn't enjoy, but one that, nevertheless, paid the bills and came with its own form of inspiration—Church was known as a gruff, complicated, and moody old man who didn't mince words and who workshopped his poems until he felt they were perfect. His ties to his friends and to the small-press scene were strong, and his mark is still lasting in those of us who read his work, corresponded with him, and drew inspiration from his words that rarely disappointed.

Dave Church died in his taxi in the early morning of Thanksgiving Day, 2008, of an apparent heart attack. His legacy is all we have left of him now, but his words will stay alive in the small press forever.

Dave: The Poet

B. Z. Niditch

from your undiscovered bed
to the rainy north
all sky is blue-hearted
by your elbow's blue door
a ragged solitude guides you
out of dusky book
to a child's deadened hunger
by red lava fields,
at your right window
apocalyptic streets of roses
butterflies echo
by bullfights and icons,
you pull your covers
of crisscrossed feathers
over a stubborn earth.

A Concealed Hour

B. Z. Niditch

A concealed hour
ages a volcano
interrogates a poet's fire.

Cold Island

B. Z. Niditch

On the cold island
words stick to branches;
a poet about the sea.

Two Guys Building a Poem

Rod Weston & Dave Church

The butterflies in my belly
Come alive before my feet
Hit the floor in the morning.

Yesterday's footprints in the snow.
A bird silent on a wire.
Today's roadmap.

In the chair by the window I wonder
Who belongs to the footprints in the snow.
The bird disappears.

The circumstances of a life
Are reflected by gray clouds.
I have for myself this moment.

Silence—
Until the bird reappears on the wire
Warbling a song.

My feathered friend reminds me
To forget about
Spies, women, intrigue.

A spider crawling up the screen
On the outside
Looking in.

Its dark eyes seem amused
At such a ghastly sight
As me.

I tap the screen.
The spider tumbles to the roof.
I wonder why I did that.

Once again I'll weave
A patchwork of coffee and smoke.
Memories fading.

Warm rain melting the snow.
May flowers pretty soon to bloom.
Butterflies in my belly fluttering still.

Good Times

Stephanie Hiteshew

in memory of Dave

Only when
I read his name
Did I believe it.
Set aside, online,
The obituary penned
His name, family,
Services—

I have a hunch
He's out with Jack,
On a rural road,
Shooting haikus,
Smoking hash,
Talking 'bout
those good times,
yeah,
those good times.

Churchman

Alan Catlin

RIP 11/27/08

I sent him a VHS copy
of *Hell Cab*, a day in the life
of a cabbie on the longest day of the year,
along with a recent *Directory of Small Press
Publishers of Poetry*

He said he didn't want to watch
a movie like that, "It was too much
like real life. Sort of like a plumber
working on pipes on his day off."

But he watched it anyway,
said it was one of the ten worst movies
he'd ever seen

He said he was starting to lose it
at work, that the long hours and the stress
of driving were killing him

He was 61

when the pen is the needle
and the paper is the spoon

Robert M. Zoschke

for Dave Church, rest in peace

today
the mailbox
offered nothing
of merit

so
I'm reading again
my postcards and letters
from Dave Church

one
of the proud true underground poets
now dead before enough people
ever got the chance to read his work

today
the mailbox
offered another
goddamn reason

why
the proud true underground poets
like Dave Church
aren't heard and read enough

glossy
promotional mailer
from what used to be
one of America's few proud true underground bookstores

WORKSHOP
the promo mailer hollers
VERBAL ROUNDABOUTS
WRITING WITH OBSESSIVE VOCABULARIES

the
workshop teacher
has a promo blurb that reeks of
rotgut academician flatulence

assistant
professor of English
teaching courses in
American poetry and creative writing

with
an MFA in poetry
and a PhD in
comparative literature

plus
the teacher published a chapbook
once
back in 2001

whoever
suffers through the godforsaken
three-hour workshop
would get more ideas worth writing about

if
they blew off the workshop
and rode around in a cab
bullshitting for three hours with the cabbie

though
they wouldn't be so lucky
to have a cabbie
like Dave Church was

it
was his hack job
driving that cab around
and Hack Job was the title of one of his books

that
hack job paid for Dave's
pen and paper and postage and electricity for his typer
and some other not-so-important things

was
an anthology with a
working title of
Alternative Voices in American Poetry since 1950

you
can bet your bottom dollar
the Verbal Roundabout Academician soon to
soil the bookstore stage isn't in there

The Streets Cry

Luis Cuauhtémoc Berriozábal

One cloud appears
in the dark sky.

Two clouds appear.
Three clouds, four more
clouds gather this

evening. A star
fills with dew and
the streets cry. I

hail a cab and
make my way home.

For Dave Church

R. Emolo

Blown-out poet dude warrior.
Older than dirty.
Taxi squad poet.
Old prune juice farts poetry.
Luck skilled bastard.
Fuck killed faster.
Fighting the landladies.
Gypsy taxi squad poet.
Rhode Island read.
Drinking toast!!!

Poem for Dave Church

A. D. Winans

I walk about the apartment
Tripping through the garden of my mind
Wandering through a luscious vertical hibernation
Beneath the quiet sheen of one light bulb
And the shadowed glow from the bedroom window
With Van Morrison and Dylan cranked beyond the
Tinnitus shaking the dust from my memory bank

I see you slumped over the steering wheel of the
Taxi cab you drove all those long years
Poet warrior who recorded my "13" jazz poems
Making the poems come alive
As no other poet could

Brought back to reality by a flock of birds
Who circle the dark clouds outside
That threaten to burst into tears
Gone but not forgotten
Jazz in your heart poetry in your soul
Your words exploding like artillery fire
Shattering the quiet of dawn

poets are like butterflies
inhabiting temporary space
tasting the pollen of life
spreading their wings
reshaping the stars the universe
cosmic matter waiting to be reborn

Indian Giver

Dave Church

for Patty on her 26th birthday

There's so much I have to say to you,
But I can't help feeling
I'm never gonna have the time—Unless it's true
That destiny doesn't trip into its grave
Before it's rightfully due.

I remember the day you first came forth.
Birth mother called me with the news.
Tears welled up inside of me and off I went
Running down the street scared and crying—
Thinking I was never gonna get to see you,
Feel you, be for you what any man
Who fathers a child should be.

All the older folks told me not to worry—
That you would be OK—Actually better off—
Seeing as how I was so young and unprepared.
Down the road in years to come they said
There would be others to take your place—
And there was.

But you stayed tucked away
In a dark corner of my mind.
And that's the part the older folks
Never said anything about—
Memories fade.
They never die.

Sometimes in the past when people would ask
How many children in the world were mine,
I raised 4 fingers to the sky.
You were always my thumb
Bent to the palm of my hand.
And now that you've come smack-dab
Back into my life—
Like the coolest shot of dope
These veins ever sucked—
Nothing anymore is invisible,
Today my raised thumb makes five.

Under a Dark Sky

Dave Church

Wonderful rain falling—
wind late September breeze—
red yellow orange leaves
crayon the earth.

Dave Church, courtesy of his daughter, Michaela Pommells.

Papa Dave

Kevin M. Hibshman

Papa Dave—
Crass,
Brash and
Beautiful,
Possessed a cab driver's wisdom and a soldier's heart
Gilded with lace and words from the street dreams of angels
You got your wings now
And I'll bet you are already singing to them.
Fierce and fuzzy Grizzly Adams with a brain,
They forgot to tell you you were mortal.

Poem for Dave Church

Glenn W. Cooper

I can't even
remember
the last poem
of yours
that I read.
No matter.
You have no
need of poetry now.
Slumped across
the dash
of your cab,
the meter still running,
the horn honking
into the still of
the night
you left
the world
of words
to the rest of us
suckers who
know not our
destination yet
run up an enormous
fare we can
never hope
to pay.

The Truth

Nathan Graziano

Your obituary in the *ProJo* reads like sheetrock.
They called you a "poet" then forgot to breathe.

I'm reading your letters, plucked from your typewriter,
my addresses ever-changing, your handwriting on the envelopes

flimsy girders stuck in the cement you called *the truth*.
The truth, old man, you cut a rug with that broad.

If you knew I was writing in couplets, you'd ask me why
then tell me to stop taking myself so fucking seriously.

You'd remind me that you gave me my first Xanax,
then allowed me to sit in your Thinking Chair,

looking out on the Providence neighborhood
where you lived, a stubborn suburb, in the attic you rented,

the slanted ceiling by the shitter, your cab parked in front
on Christmas Eve, a dusting of snow on the windshield,

both of us drinking instant coffee after a long night
out dueling each other at the bar, smoking a joint

in the parking lot outside the scope of the floodlights.
Later, your son met up with us, and he recited a poem

you wrote, and goddamn, you should've seen your face
scorched with pride. I did. And there it was: *the truth*.

Hey, old man, it's not yet noon and already I want a beer,
but you once told me to never start drinking before 2 p.m.

and I'm going to try to honor that rule, then crack
the first one for you, my friend, because you wouldn't want

a poem as a tribute, nor an obituary that dazzled.
Just *the truth*. And that's about as honest as I get these days.

Under Stars

Luis Cuauhtémoc Berriozábal

Under stars,
the kind stars,
you are free.
You need nothing.
Simple life
is a gift.
There is hope
and there is light.
You are free.
Your wrists are
not being
bound by a chain.
You must live
Breathe the air.
The kind stars
watch over you.

The *Barbaric Yawp* Interview: June 2002

John Berbrich & Dave Church

JOHN BERBRICH: What happened the last time somebody stiffed you for a cab fare?

DAVE CHURCH: The last time I got stiffed for a cab ride happened two weeks before Christmas. Two young kids hailed me down next to the Greyhound bus station. The sun was just coming up. They wanted to go to a place called Clown Town on the south side. They call it Clown Town because every house on the street is painted either pink, yellow, purple, or green. We got to their house, and the meter read ten dollars. The two kids got out of the cab and started walking inside. I called out to them about the money they owed. One of the kids nonchalantly turned around and said, "Man, I ain't got no money." Then they disappeared. I sat there for a minute thinking if I should have the dispatcher call the cops. Then I started to chuckle with amusement. The whole scene, the way it all went down, suddenly didn't matter. I was taken for a ride and didn't mind. I mean, those two kids walked away in style. I almost admired them. Then I just drove away. On another note, it was to their advantage that I was in a pretty good mood at that moment in time.

JB: Did you write a poem about it?

DC: No, I didn't write a poem about it. The ingredients are certainly there to make one, but I rarely, if ever, draw inspiration anymore from anything that happens in the taxi. But that could change at any time. Right now you've got me thinking about those two kids. Funny how poems get born.

JB: When did you start driving a cab?

DC: I started driving a cab in 1988.

JB: Why?

DC: Well, prior to that year, I was in the home-improvement business—roofing, siding, painting, and carpentry. I was making big bags of money. The IRS had a see at my books in 1987. They didn't like what they saw. After the audit, they determined that I owed them forty-thousand bucks. According to the plan they set up for me, I was to pay them back at the rate of five-hundred dollars a week. According to the plan I set up for myself, I would go from making big bags of money to making hardly any money at all. I figured by suddenly turning into a pauper, they would eventually leave me alone. Eventually they did, but not before I went to my share of meetings with agents trying to put the squeeze on me. I always made it a point to wear shabby clothing when attending these meetings. I would also smoke a big fat joint beforehand. This caused me to drift in and out of the conversation—giving the appearance of someone suffering from attention deficit disorder. And other times I would ramble on about things that had nothing to do with why I was there. The last agent was so confused, she felt sorry for me and filed my case for a year. That was about five years ago. I still get an occasional letter from them, but I think they've pretty much written me off as a dead-beat loser—which is OK by me. Getting a job driving a cab was the vehicle I used to put such a plan into motion.

JB: Have you written a lot of IRS poems?

DC: Only one, but it's still in the wash. It's been there for two years. It's still there because I can't get it clean enough to put in the dryer. Let me explain. The phrase, still in the wash, means the poem is incomplete—still in the womb, so to speak. If and when the poem ever gets born, I transfer it to an incubator—a folder marked Drying Out. The drying out phase is when the poem matures. You can call it the adolescent stage of development. I check in on these poems from time to time to see how they look and feel. Sometimes I make minor adjustments. Sometimes I return them to the wash. When completely dry, I let them fly. Some find a home, and some return in the form of a rejection letter. Now you have me thinking about that poem. Maybe today I'll visit it to see if I can induce labor. If anything good happens, you'll be the first to know.

JB: Hey, have you written a poem about your method of composition—the conception, birth, et cetera? A lot of great metaphors there.

DC: I wrote a poem once about sitting at the typer listening to the hum of its idle—waiting on the poem, so to speak. But that isn't how I approach the poem—although it does happen from time to time. My method is to write the first thought down exactly as it comes to me. With that thought might come another, and then another. Time passes. At any given time, depending on my mood, I'll sift through my notebooks looking for a scribble or two or three that might give me an idea, or a feel for a poem that translates into a first draft. From there, it develops as I explained in my answer to your previous question. I don't have much faith in Ginsberg's proclamation that the first thought is the best thought, therefore, we should ride that thought through the moment it's happening right on to the finish line. For as simple as my poems appear on the page, I do many revisions—paying special attention to word choice, the placement of these words to create a form complementing the rhythm of the poem. Then of course there is content. I always ask myself the big question—is the poem unique and significant? Most of the time it isn't—but I keep on trying.

JB: I've heard several recordings of you reading your poetry. Exactly who are The Wrinkles?

DC: I have no idea who The Wrinkles are. I found the tape in a box with a bunch of others belonging to my landlady. The minute I heard the music, I knew I had no choice but to make a recording. It's perfect for the humorous and "tongue in cheek" poem. You say you've heard several of my spoken word performances. Here, check out this CD, *BeBop ReBop.*

JB: Thanks. That's funny—I had imagined The Wrinkles as this cool blues-rock band, playing seedy joints in Providence. Do you ever read poetry backed by live music?

DC: I gave my first poetry reading in 1975 at a place here in Providence called Lupo's Heartbreak Hotel. I was backed by a group of musicians playing piano, sax, drums, stand-up bass, electric guitar, and a chick who looked like Cher with a tambourine. We had that "gig" every Sunday afternoon throughout the spring and summer. Someone would always pass the hat. We usually made enough money to cover our bar tab—which was pretty substantial. For the next two years, I did readings at local colleges, public parks, high schools, and lots of saloons. I even read once at a pizza parlor. I was always accompanied by a musician who played either drums or acoustic guitar—sometimes both. By the time the seventies came to a close, I had dropped out of the poetry scene altogether. When I returned in 1990, I did a few readings on my own before hooking up with a band called the Flying Ditch Diggers. They were a hard-working band, so I got to play some pretty decent crowds around town and beyond. We all went separate ways when the band broke up around 1995. I don't read with musical accompaniment anymore—at least not live.

JB: If reincarnation is a thing, what would you like to come back as?

DC: If reincarnation is a THING, and we believe what Sartre says—that a thing (an object) has being, but not existence, as opposed to man, who does—then I would like to come back as a seat on a stationary bicycle in a women's health spa in Hollywood. Either that or a bra belonging to a hot young movie star.

JB: No, no, Dave—that sounds like heaven, not an Earthly reincarnation. But okay then, what do you think heaven would be like?

DC: That's a tough question for someone who doesn't believe in heaven. But since I don't know for sure—remember, where there is belief, there is no knowledge—I'd like to think that heaven would be a place where people just sit around feeding the birds—or better yet—turn into one.

JB: Speaking hypothetically—what sort of bird would you turn into?

DC: Any bird that lives in a tropical rainforest. I love rain and would rather be heard than seen. In a tropical rainforest, that's the way it is with birds. They don't really fly the sky all that much. They mostly stay in the trees and sing. And food is plentiful.

JB: Speaking of songbirds, who are some of your favorite poets warbling from the limbs of the small press these days?

DC: Favorite poets of the small press is a tough question simply because there are so many to choose from. For the girls, I'd have to say Ann Menebroker for the way she gives meaning to so many things we take for granted in life, Lynne Savitt for raw sexual honesty, and Linda Lerner for her energy. A few guys I like are Ray Mason for his clever irony—not to mention humor. Catfish McDaris is another poet who makes me laugh. He can also pen some pretty good tender love songs. I'd add Dan Crocker to that mix, as well. I could go on and on, but enough is enough.

JB: What do you think of the position of Poet Laureate in the USA?

DC: I compare the position of Poet Laureate in the USA to the position of Poet Laureate for the city of Providence, Rhode Island, where I live. He's squeaky clean and a member in good standing with the local community of artists. In other words, he participates in the practice of raising money to fund the various projects he determines important—like the annual trip to whatever city is hosting the national poetry slam contest that he just happens to be a part of. He helps assemble the team of poets who will represent the city and serves as their coach. He was appointed to this position by the mayor—who is now on trial in federal court for allegedly running a criminal enterprise. Does that answer your question?

JB: What do you think of our present Poet Laureate, Billy Collins?

DC: As for Billy Collins, I first became aware of him five years ago in the *American Poetry Review*. He writes like he's sitting across from you at a table over coffee and just telling a story that gets to the point without all that highbrow rhetoric that's so dense and basically—for me at least—unreadable. I don't know much about what he's done as the Poet Laureate.

JB: Okay, Dave, this is it. Do you have any final comments or observations—philosophical, literary, or otherwise—for the folks at home?

DC: Heave Ho your cheap possessions. Pay attention to the flies in the eyes of the children.

Dave Church, courtesy of his daughter, Michaela Pommells.

Editors: Wants and Needs (Update 2009)

David S. Pointer

idea based on the fine original by Jon Taylor

Nothing Wallace Stevens or
Lyn Lifshin might have penned.
No Dave Church clones. No
Bukowski hacks or hackettes.
No poems with poetry in them.
Nothing from the Beat school.
Definitely no Black Mountain
or experimental. No tag-team
haiku hacking unless prearranged
by our German editor in Switzerland.
No circle hacks. Would like to see
more eco-friendly non-nature poems.
The guest editor would like to see
more middle-of-the-road edge poems.
No sainted granny poems unless your
grandma drinks Blue Thong martinis. ...
I guess the only things left to mail
are muse magic, truth, and passion.

Tribute

Jonathan Church

I have what one may deem a "naturalistic" view of life and death. Flesh and blood are all I can apprehend, and in this realm of apprehension, death is the very end of consciousness. It's final. The heart beats no more.

I do not deny that the life of a man has a destination that follows his direct encounter with the face of death, but this destination is a place that seems only to be reached during our life on earth by a so-called leap of faith. And so it is that notions of spirituality and religious transcendence have no resonance for me. I'm only affected, or moved, by what I can apprehend with my rational and empirical faculties. Notions of spirituality and religious transcendence, or simply the idea of an afterlife, are beyond the reach of these faculties, and as a result, they do not resonate with me. I have not the legs for a leap of faith.

This is partly the result of having studied evolution, which provided me with a peculiar comfort rooted in the wonder of a world of order, but without design, or some meta-human moral bedrock. This is the comfort of attaching no more moral or ethereal significance to human life than to any other form of life. Putting aside biological notions of kin selection and the like, there is no moral hierarchy in my view of life and nature.

This is a comfort to me because one cannot help but accept death as being in the natural order of things. There is no God's plan to question, or in which to find disappointment and anger. Death does not discriminate. It comes to us all.

Now, I am not here to question faith, or to advance the cause of nihilism. I am perfectly capable of being a believer. It is simply to say that I find the meaning in life in the relationships we develop with our family, friends, society, and the environment to which our bodies are adapted. It is these relationships that fuel the contents of our consciousness. And this is why death can hurt so much. It is in death that we see what is really true about our lives.

Death takes away the conversations with a consciousness with which we shared our conceits. All we have left is to remember the times, and in doing so to pretend that we can speak for him, as if to say, "Oh, what David would have said about that ...," and then proceed under the pretense that we can say what he would have said. But doubt lingers in this pretense, for only Dave Church could be Dave Church. Death forbids this carcass to correct me as I try to make sense of the life he once lived. Anything I say about Dave Church is most likely inaccurate. "Words, words, words ...," as Hamlet said. And that is the simple tragedy of death: that he is gone, and I can no longer enjoy talking to him, being in his presence, and having him say what is to be said in his own words.

Nevertheless, I am left to speak of his legacy in my own words, in the best way I can. Now, I have conveyed this view of life and death not simply to take the pulpit and explain how evolution has influenced my thinking, but because this view speaks to his legacy in the sense that it is the result of being the son of Dave Church. My father once said that we are all the same when we are asleep, which I suppose can mean a lot of things, but in this setting I take the liberty of believing that he and I saw eye to eye in the belief that we are one among many millions and billions of creatures who live and have lived, and all are of equal interest to the poet's empathetic eye. It is no coincidence, then, that he was once compelled to write a poem called "Joe the Bee" about a bumblebee slowly descending into death after being smothered in paint.

More than anything else, Dave Church was a poet, and those first fires of poetic feeling were ignited in 1965, when he read a book called *Why I Am Not a Christian* by Bertrand Russell, and books such as *A Coney Island of the Mind* by Lawrence Ferlinghetti. From that point on, Dave Church was a poet, and a poet doomed, as were the people who would come to know him.

He was difficult, but it is this quality that gave his life its charm, that made it mysterious, that, in the end, stirred our feelings about him, whatever they may have been. Bob Dylan has a song in which he says: "Strange how people who suffer together have stronger connections than people who are most content." Dave Church was a difficult man—difficult to live with, difficult to get along with, and difficult to understand. He was stubborn, cantankerous, irascible, and capable of the most stinging of insults and offenses. One did not participate in his life without a degree of suffering, whether it was his conceits, his moods, or his prejudices. But in that suffering, strong connections were made.

Here's a quick story: my mother and father were having one

of their many, many arguments one night, and at one point my father slammed his fist against a portrait of a ballerina that my mother had recently purchased, to which my mother replied, "You just destroyed a beautiful work of art!" To which Dave Church replied, "No, now it's a work of art, because now it has passion!"

So, getting back to my theme, my view of life and death is not the same as a disbelief in immortality, or even simply life after death. It is simply a view that flesh and blood have no other destination than disintegration, but the passions that once stirred in this flesh and blood live on, in his writings, and in the memory of those who were lucky, or unlucky, enough to fall into the stew of his life.

It's always hard to describe the relationships one has had with people, for words are such feeble tools for getting access to the stew of emotions and thoughts mixed together in the sorcery of a complex relationship. But I believe that the essence of his relationships was his uncensored, honest-to-goodness passion, for Dave Church had a way of really letting you know how he felt. It's not so simple to say merely that he loved, or hated, certain people. I believe that he did, both love and hate, but saying so only cheapens the suffering he felt when he truly confronted the passions within him.

I was sad to realize that he would never get to experience a wish he had related to me one time: that he would have liked to have all his kids together in one place at one time. I told this to Courtney the other day, and she remembered that she made that offer to him a few years ago, to which he replied that he wasn't in the mood.

Different people will hear that story and sneer, groan, sigh, and smirk. But I laughed. It was vintage Dave Church.

Not sure when Courtney asked him, but my guess is it would have been close to a workday, before or, more likely, after. He hated the taxi industry, even if he could not help but empathize with and write about the seedy netherworld that he witnessed from behind the wheel. And a long night of driving wore him down, affected his mood, and left him disgusted. I'd ask him on a Sunday morning, so how's the cab business, and he'd say, "It sucks." I'd ask him, so how's Providence, and he'd say, "It sucks." But on a good day, he'd still tell me something about the night, like the dancer he was mentoring like a surrogate father; or the kids who called him Santa and asked where Mrs. Claus is, to which he replied, "She's at home sucking your mother's cunt"; or the cop who asked him not to park his car in front of a bar where he wanted to wait for potential customers, so that he started to drive back and forth on the street waving to the cop every time he drove by in a kind of tragicomic mockery; or the guy who was drunk and gave him a $50 bill by accident, which he kept for himself (justifying his actions by recalling the time that he went into a bar the night before his wedding to his third wife, dropped a $100 bill on the bar, put his head down, fell asleep, and woke up to find the $100 bill vanished).

Dave Church was a man who deferred to his moods without inhibition. Expressing his contempt for anti-depressants and other self-help substances, he said he would prefer to feel his depression, internalize and understand it (which, by the way, is not to say that he was not capable of drugging himself up with anti-depressants if it suited his mood). But back to Courtney's story: a long night of driving, or writing, whatever it might have been, there were times of recovery for him, and these are times when he would not be bothered. The moment simply had to be right, and he was stubborn enough to insist on it. It wasn't even a matter of principle. For a man of such passion, his heart simply had to be in it at the moment.

I've given you some vignettes of his life, but the overall impression I would like to leave is my belief, and it is only my belief, that he suffered in his passions, and that the grandest passion for him was love, the four letters of which were tattooed to his right forearm. He suffered because there were moments when he relived and contemplated the suffering he caused for himself and among those he truly loved. He once wrote a letter to his daughter Tara in the mid-80s after a fight one night, in which he said the following:

> I'm sorry for what I said and did
> Last night.
> When I drink too much I become
> Obnoxious and insensitive
> I want you to stay with me
> Because I love you
> I want you to become a success
> Whatever that means
> In many ways I guess I feel guilty
> Of failing you
> If I have
> Then I'm sorry

But either way
Without sounding stupidly redundant
I love you

He wrote letters and poems to and about his other children, his wives, his siblings, other family, and his friends. At this point, I don't know how many, and how many of the many have been preserved. I don't want to keep us here all day, so I will only say that he never censored his passions. This was the source of our suffering with him, and because we suffered, he suffered. He suffered, I believe, because deep down, where it really mattered, he truly loved. And I believe that for no other reason than the quality of his poetry, which has become apparent to me with the outpouring I have received from the community of poets he knew around the country.

Gerry Nicosia, biographer of Jack Kerouac, wrote: "Now no more Dave to chat with, in that gruff raspy heart-of-gold voice of his (a sort of Walter Matthau with an East Coast accent, I used to think), to send poems and funny stories and wry political quips and cartoons back and forth with. I only met him once, when he drove up to Boston to hear me give a reading off Harvard Square with the poet Buddah. But your dad was one of the most decent guys I ever met. And a damn fine poet."

And there have been many others, and it seems they will continue to pour in. And that is one reason I held his hand and kissed his forehead when I was alone with his body in the hospital morgue. I truly loved him, as a father, friend, writer, and most of all, as a man.

What I'll miss about him the most is that he was a man who just knew where it's at. For example, I received a letter from one of his friends in the poetry community, who related a line from his last letter: "If it's not one thing, it's another. You just have to know how to duck."

It's hard not to know where things stand in life, when your best friend's face is scrambled raw dripping from shattered glass after a car accident, when another best friend is found one day dead from hanging, when your young sister dies in a car accident at the hands of a drunk driver, when your brother burns to death while sleeping in the woods, when your older sister dies of cancer, when you've spent time in a chain gang, when another friend stabs you some thirty times in the face and neck and then, in the true spirit of schizophrenia, drives you to the hospital emergency room, and on and on.

Dave Church knew suffering, and as a result, I believe, he had a way of reading and empathizing with people. Not saying it was necessarily accurate, but it was raw, it was uncensored, and it was unedited. And that is what made him the artist that he was.

He was real. He was eccentric, difficult, stubborn, disagreeable, but more than anything ... alone, a gentle poetic soul, alone in his unease for the demands of respectable society. Maladaptive, yes, but it was true to form—a life of fiction, a bit like Dean Moriarty in Kerouac's *On the Road*, or the junkie Herbert Huncke, or the poet he loved most, Gregory Corso. And with that, I will read a short poem of mine, which I don't claim to make any sense:

Remember the Time

Jonathan Church

The end of time is here,
With naught but the past
Upon which to ruminate,
For the future shall be no more
As the sun sets on longing,
Ambition replaced by nostalgia
Or, even better, death,
When a life of ceaseless toil
To conquer one's time and place
Comes to its natural end,

And so it is that we must accept
The wrinkles of our quest
To wrestle with the tides of time
Until the riddle has been ridiculed,

And life becomes no more
Than a long night of rest

Dave Church, courtesy of his daughter, Michaela Pommells.

Before You Let Go

Dave Church

Take them when their hands are small
To pick and save those special stones
In the bed of a stream, seashells
From the ocean floor.

Take them when their hands are small
To fondle the bud of a rose;
Catch sight of the butterfly,
The robin in the bird bath.

Take them when their hands are small
To wander the forests
And meadows
In the wilderness of night.

Take them when their hands are small
To ride a winged horse,
Reach for the chariot
Riding the sky.

Take them when their hands are small
To wade in the water
At the river's edge
Hold on tight.

God Is in the Cab

Steve Dalachinsky

for your return address
these past 2 years
you put:

GOD
30 Forest St.
Providence R.I.

now   R.I.(P.)
  as Providence would have
you ...
pickin' up yer last fare
with yer heart
somewhere in the "... forest
of the Night"

up there right now
playin' God to a host of passengers
in yer Technicolor Cab
pickin' up hookers 'n hustlers 'n
gangsters 'n lefties 'n righties
'n poets 'n drunkards 'n petty thieves ...

tellin' us "hippies" we should be
grateful for the free rides

speakin' out like the music on
Main Street
wingin' wishes just off the right
of Center
"tougher than bone or wood"
warm man/child
father lover plain talker
teller of like it is

funny eye/cat speakin' thru
the jive
i owe you a lunch
   / you owe me a book
a visit
   a letter /
           savin' on postage does not
  make me happy right now
       this has been a month of heart
    attacks & suicides
          & politics as usual
              no matter what the believers
               may think
but you crew-mate dreamer behind that macho mask
    righteous gentleman are here with me now
          returning my words.

Dave Church:
A Providence Poet

B. Z. Niditch

his energy and poetry
kept you up at night
like old ice
for his fifth drink
swearing a day for happiness
you will not enter
a friend's house
or say Mass or Kaddish
for a lost soul
here in the rain
the world is wounded
and thunder pours out
her refrain
for one so golden in his bed.

To Construct a Blues

Herschel Silverman

for David Church

OPEN WITH SAD EARTH PAIN-LINE
BOW DOWN HEAD AND PRAY
SEARCH THRU LYRICS IN MIND
BEAT OUT HOMEGROWN NOTES
GLIMPSE WALLS TO WAIL AGAINST
WAILS TO HANG BLUES ON
PEEK THRU BLUE SHADES
SEE ROSE PETALS FALL OFF GRAND ILLUSIONS
CLIMB MOUNTAIN OF BABEL
WITH DRUM SAX VIBRAPHONE CLARINET

TIME OPENS ITS DRAWER
PULLS OUT BLUES WITH MEMORY
TRANSCRIPTIONS OF BLUE CONSTRUCTIONS
VISIONS   VISIONS   VISIONS   VISIONS
OLD VIBRATIONS
SKY FLIES BLUE
BLUE VIBRAPHONE STORM
EVERYTHING IS RELEVANT
OFF-KEY ALLITERATIONS
REVELATIONS   CONSTERNATIONS
EARLY SPRING WILL BLOSSOM
MIST OF SORROW FALLS ON SOUL
FOG IS HITCHED TO RUNAWAY STARS

NITE EARTH SHUFFLES ITS JOKERS
DRUM BEATS OUT INEVITABLE BLUES
CLARINET WAILS THRU BOWERY POETRY
THRU CITYSCAPE   THRU ZEITGEIST
THRU HAMPELLING
FUTURE IS WELDED BLUE
BOW DOWN HEAD AND PRAY
CLOSE EYES ON SAD EARTH PAIN-LINE
CONSTRUCT A BLUES   CONSTRUCT A BLUES

Dave Church, R. I. P.

Nathan Graziano

Last night, while I was staying at my parents' place in Rhode Island, I received news via email that the Rhode Island poet, and my friend, Dave Church, had passed away at age 61. It has been years since I've spoken to Dave—or corresponded with him through letters, which was our primary line of communication—yet the news hit me hard.

During the years of 2001-2002, I would receive long letters from Dave, typed on his old electric typewriter, and fire letters back zealously. Today, when I returned home to New Hampshire, I went through a box of personal items—poems and stories I've written that never saw a second draft and many of my old letters from writers, friends, ex-girlfriends, etc. Since the dawn of our technological age, emails seem to have made the art of the epistolary form obsolete; and digging up Dave Church's old letters and reading through them this afternoon, soaking up the wisdom, heart, and honesty that went into them, it seems to me that this is *more* than a damn shame.

Maybe some other time I'll write about my experiences visiting Dave in his attic apartment in Providence, the characters and improbable episodes that unfolded, but right now, it doesn't seem right to eulogize him with fancy or funny anecdotes. I can, however, say this: I learned as much, if not more, about life and writing from talking and corresponding with Dave Church than I have in most of my MFA workshop classes (and I've had some fabulous workshop professors). Sadly, for the last half-decade, Dave and I lost touch, and consequently, I missed out on an education, at a time when I most needed his perspective. I want to include a poem that Dave sent me in a letter dated 8-14-02—every one of Dave's letters came to me with poems, fliers for readings, or audio tapes. ... It seems to me, right now, to be especially apropos:

And I'm the Star

Dave Church

The same movie has been playing in my head
for three nights now. It's called
THIS IS YOUR LIFE!

In the beginning
there's plenty of action—
fast cars,
easy money,
a babe on both
sides of me,
and two
on my lap.

The middle moves along
in an ordinary way.
The action is packed
with more corn
than pop.

It's the ending that bothers me—

I'm falling ...

Searching for Parts

Dave Church & Steve Dalachinsky

Under the seat
Of the wrecked car
An eyeball.

It stared straight at
My crotch.
Its gender? A fragment
Of the senses.

It winked!
I thought by that gesture
It meant me no harm.

Winks can be deceiving.
As are smiles cut like knives
On a summer night.

True!
But it's December and cold.
Yet my fingertips melt like the
Ice caps themselves.

If that be the case,
Buy a bag of ice cubes
Or cut off your hands
& handle that camera carefully
When entering the subway.

Does the eyeball have a camera?
Maybe eyeballs on the subway too ...
Sketching distances between passengers
All seeing & lidless
Like a fish.

blizzard

T. Kilgore Splake

for Dave Church

strange reason
my cuppa
green tea
tastes great
this early a.m.

Dave Church (1947-2008)

George Held

Opening the envelope containing the fall 2008 *Barbaric Yawp*, I first took a look at its newsletter, "From the Marrow," and my eyes lit upon the phrase "the late Dave Church" as a contributor to *Free Verse*. I was shocked and needed confirmation. Before looking for the editor's phone number, I first checked out the bio notes in the *Yawp* and saw an editorial insertion in Dave's bio note, saying he'd died of a heart attack on Thanksgiving Day. Then I checked the last letter he'd written me and saw that it's dated November 17, 2008—ten days before Thanksgiving.

I was overdue to answer it. Dave and I had for the past ten years exchanged one or two letters per month, commenting on the small-press scene, sympathizing over our many rejections and other disappointments in po' biz, and trying out new poems and short stories on each other. Occasionally a published poem would be the result of our silent collaboration. In his last letter, by the way, he mentions the six poems the *Yawp*'s editor included in the October issue: "John B|erbrich| from the *YAWP* wrote to tell me he would be publishing a bunch of short poems I sent him in the next issue. What I sent him was not a submission, but a sampling of poems for |a| possible book." That book ms. and probably dozens of unpublished poems constitute part of Dave's considerable legacy.

Judging from the memorial comments I've read online, Dave was much admired and will be greatly missed. He corresponded with a number of other poets, and a collection of his letters would chronicle, in his caustic yet deadpan way, the small-press poetry scene of the past 25 years. His letters to me were full of evaluations of other poets and brickbats aimed at those he considered frauds, hustlers, or wannabes. He also didn't suffer dilatory editors easily: "I no longer cut these publishers any slack. If they don't respond within the time stated in their guidelines (with a two-week grace period), I'll resubmit elsewhere. I don't care anymore. And fuckem if they don't like it. They're not paying me." His indignation was earned by decades of presence in the small-press world and his fundamental sense of fair play. He also had a wry sense of humor that made his letters, like many of his short stories and poems, highly entertaining. If he was at times irascible, as one online memorial claims, it was because he honored poetry so much that he lost patience with those for whom writing poems was a therapeutic mind-game or a means of self-aggrandizement.

We first started corresponding when, in the late '90s, he wrote to ask me to send him some poems for an anthology of underground American poets that he hoped to edit. In 2000, he printed a few of my poems in *Full Circle*, the occasional broadside he published on his own dime from Represst Publishing, in Providence, the city he inhabited for the past few decades. It was where he set up shop as a bard who supported himself as a hack, a word he loved for its slangy authenticity and the irony of its reference to him as a "hack" writer. But as his collection of short stories, *Hack Job* (2002), shows, he was a writer who took himself as seriously as he deserved, but not too seriously. A series of vignettes of the life of a Providence taxi driver, the collection shows him to have mastered the short-short story as deftly as he had the short poem. In what might have been one of his own scenarios, he died at the wheel as he waited for help after his Checker cab had broken down.

Dave was originally a dairy farmer, working on the family spread in Rhode Island. He had also been a teenage vagabond and was later a house painter in Providence, before he became a cab driver. The mix of jobs and his travels proved more valuable to him as a poet than a degree in creative writing.

As the editor says in his *Yawp* bio note, Dave had recently been writing a lot of short nature poems, many based on the haiku, like the six printed in the said issue. He was able to switch from his mostly urban poems to haiku, because he had no set agenda for his poetry: he found a subject wherever he looked, and his eyes were always keenly open. His openness to subjects and poetic forms made him an original, as did his ornery, independent outlook on life, politics, mores, and poetry itself. He both resisted and rejected classification. Though some might see him as a neo-Beat, a descendant of Bukowski, or a street poet, he eluded any such categories and he was critical of all of them.

Because it eludes any particular school of poetry, the element in a poem he valued most was what he called "mouth-feel," which he mentions in his blurb for my chapbook *Grounded*. "Mouth-feel," he told me, is the quality of writing that makes a poem sound and feel natural when read aloud, and that quality might be found among poets either known or obscure. Rare as it is, "mouth-feel" resonates in at least one of those last six nature poems in *Barbaric Yawp*:

> Dark sunrise.
> Last night's fog and rain,
> Lingering.

This brief lyric speaks for no school, except maybe the ancient one of Basho, whose classical simplicity it recalls. Neither Beat, Buk, nor Street, this is just plain great poetry. These words, and many others uttered and authored by Dave Church, will linger at least as long as we do.

Dave Church, drawn and painted by Henry Denander.

By Life

Stephanie Hiteshew

We woke
One less.

Notebook
Empty

Stamps left
Out

Pages upon
Pages

Of
Poems

Without
Finished lines

Taken by life
And its alternate self.

Giving Thanks

Luis Cuauhtémoc Berriozábal

I have corresponded
with many poets
in the past 10 years
or so. I always
feel bad when I hear
one of the poets
I have shared friendly
words with died. I
feel especially bad
hearing about Dave
Church dying on
Thanksgiving Day
and even worse
because I had never
corresponded with
him. I always read
his poems and was
never disappointed.
I wish I had let Dave
know how much his
words meant to me.
This poem is the only way
I know how to thank him.

News That Burns On

David S. Pointer

Tell me Dave Church
is reading under a
magnificent cast brass
Spanish chandelier
receiving coins and
mass congratulations
or that he's borrowing
an old Mohawk Martin
fly reel catching fat
mountain trout then
fending off hot lot
lizards with way too
many hits from Prohibition
era Anheuser-Busch
beer or that he's
studying a winking
man star in prestorm
skies plucking great words
to describe taxi cab
crash parts to a grateful
group in a luminous pub.

I Am Water

Dave Church & Steve Dalachinsky

I am water in the stream
running to the river
that flows to the sea
from where I came
to where I'll disappear
cooking legal stuff with the fishes
delivering unlimited toppings every 35 minutes
because safety is a priority
& within my house visions are always scenic
yet tho I am liquid
my thirst is never quenched

What about breast milk?
BREAST MILK!
It trains the eye to linger at wanderers
with swollen tongues. Boycott baby formula!
Eat it raw ...

more than this eye-boned eyeburn
the sun blocking out the shades in her profile
green is the trash of this century
disguised as salvation

drink the thick milk of seals
squeeze it from their bellies as the sign
you won't find your head
on a park bench
nor blue sky nor
river of PISS.

Gilbert

Dave Church

first draft, as sent to T. Kilgore Splake

He's gone now—
Ashes to wind,
To dust.

No longer here to ponder
The flow of the stream,
The push and pull
Of ocean tides,
The flight of birds
On the wing.

No longer here to ponder
The shadows in the day
Or night,
The lilies
In the valley of death,
The mystery of morning star,
The face of the man in the moon.

No longer here to listen
To the tap tapping of the rain,
The orchestra in timberland,
The wind on a breeze
Or gust of storm.

He's gone now—
Far from the waters of Babylon,
The loaves of wisdom he cast
Float in waiting now
For those he left behind.
His crown of thorns ripped
And scattered—
Ashes too
To wind,
To dust.

Far away he goes now,
Far away he goes—

My brother,
On the road atop a camel—

The eye of the needle
So very near to thread.

Hack Poet

George Held

for Dave Church

You drove whenever—
Nights, holidays, hurricanes—
Your notebook beside you
To receive a new idea
For poem or story whenever
It came to you

Till last Thanksgiving, when
Your hack came to a stop
With your last heart-thump.
Every passenger
In the small press
Mourns your loss.

Dave Church, drawn and
painted by Henry Denander.

God's lonely man

Leah Angstman

His last laugh in
this brooding world a
death on a day of
giving thanks,

a taxi seemingly getting
smaller,
tighter,
less room for explosions
of mind and body,
a poor place for genius
and burial

but a daily footprint
filled of one who
died with his foot
still in the shoe.

Acknowledgments

"Two Guys Building a Poem" and "Good Times" were previously published in *Cokefishing in Alpha Beat Soup* January 2009.

"Under a Dark Sky" was previously published in *Cranial Tempest*.

"The *Barbaric Yawp* Interview: June 2002" was previously published in *Barbaric Yawp* Vol. 6, No. 2.

"God Is in the Cab," "To Construct a Blues," "Searching for Parts," "By Life," and "I Am Water" were simultaneously published in R. Emolo's Dave Church memoriam broadside.

"Dave Church, R.I.P." was previously published on Nathan Graziano's blog.

"Dave Church (1947-2008)" was previously published on the *New York Quarterly Poets* website.

Dedication

For Dave
and all the small-press poets who have passed,
read or unread

Billy and Cindy
by

Stephanie Hiteshew
and
Dave Church

Billy & Cindy

Stephanie Hiteshew
& Dave Church

Introduction by
Stephanie Hiteshew, 2009

In late 1996, Billy and Cindy began a series of letter writing that carried their relationship through the cold streets of Rhode Island and of Baltimore. It is within their letters that this story takes place.

*

Billy & Cindy—the sequel to the prose book *Hack Job*, written by the late Dave Church—was written by both Dave Church and Stephanie Hiteshew over the last two years of Dave's life. Sadly, Dave Church passed away on Thanksgiving day, 2008.

City Love

Stephanie Hiteshew

Wrote you a letter
said all those things:
how love in the city
fends off leaving you just a statistic,
greets you at the subway station and
buys you a coffee.

That love takes its toll
when limits bend too far;
that sex doesn't mean marriage,
that streets hold different roads.

Smelled your coffee on the way to work;
carried you with me all day
no matter the weather.

Some nights I wanted time
considering your photo growing dust on my shelf,
three years since being placed there by both of us.

Looked in the mailbox
and found your hastily written letter.
Return address unlisted,
I tucked it in my totebag.

Caught the metro to the city park;
sat on the bench, where we first met.
Unopened, I ripped up your letter.

In the morning, the city will find me again,
and like the ocean's undertow, pull me in.

Part One

Dear Billy,

I'm in Baltimore. Sorry I didn't let you know sooner. Anyway, I'm thinking seriously about coming back. Everywhere I look, girls are getting beat up. Johns are getting busted. A new breed of young thugs are taking over the streets. It's really bad.

If I stay around here, there is no way for me to avoid that scene. Billy, I'm 38 years old, and tired. Tired of screwing up my life. I know I can do better. Besides, I can't stop thinking about you; all alone up there in Providence.

I don't have a lot of money right now, but that will change in a hurry. You know me. I'm wondering if maybe I could stay with you just until I find a place. I know it's a lot to ask, but I'll make it up to you in more ways than one—and you know what I mean.

I hope to hear from you soon.

You can reach me at:
P.O. Box 618,
Baltimore City, MD 21201

Love,
Cindy

June 1, 1996

Dear Cindy,

I thought you were dead. Why did you wait six months to contact me? And why did you disappear in the first place like dust in the wind? Whatever, I'm glad you're thinking about coming back to Providence. I miss you, too.

No, I don't mind if you stay with me while you look to get settled. I'm moving out of this crummy room above the liquor store at the end of the month. Found a decent place on the east side about a mile from Brown University. Four rooms with heat and electricity included. It's not cheap, but affordable—as long as I stay glued to the seat behind the wheel of the cab. I can't wait. If I live in this blood-stained neighborhood any longer, I'm gonna snap.

So, if you can hold on for three more weeks I'll be ready for you. Who knows, it might turn into a permanent arrangement. But what's a 60-year-old burned-out cab driver gonna do with a young "filly" like you—unless the obvious answer is enough.

Write soon and let me know if my plan will match up with yours. Hope you're going easy with the drug thing. I'm still guzzling a few beers now and then. No pot! Can't believe all the money I used to spend on that stuff. Not writing much at all. Hard to concentrate. Thoughts blow in and out of my head faster than speeding bullets.

My P.O. Box number will remain the same for now.

Looking forward ...
Billy

June 6, 1996

Dear Billy,

It's good to hear from you and know that you are doing well. I went ahead and bought a train ticket to Providence for June 29th. You said three weeks, right? I'm so relieved that you can help me. Court was brutal, but it all turned out O.K.

I can't believe you think age sixty is old! I've seen what you can do, and believe me, you still rock it like those young bucks.

I'm O.K. with the drug thing. I've been straight for thirty days. Thirty-three to be exact. No night sweats or vomiting in weeks. I feel good about myself for the first time in a long time.

The other day I was thinking of my mother. She told me years ago I'd find a man, but he'd be much older. She said, "Older men know more about life and can do a lot more in bed." That's my mother for you: wisdom and sex. Rumor has it she was talented—if you know what I mean. Maybe she was psychic, too.

When I get up there with you, I'll start working as soon as I can. With the extra money, you'll finally have the time you need to write. I know how important that is to you. I'm sorry I disappeared, Billy. Things happen, and I lose track of what I'm doing. I'm good now. I have a game plan. You'll be proud of me.

Write soon.

Your main squeeze,
Cindy

June 11, 1996

Dear Cindy,

O.K.! June 29th. Plan your arrival in the evening so I can pick you up in the cab. I called the new landlord hoping he'd tell me the apartment would be ready a few days early. No luck. I guess I can always rent a hotel room for a few nights. We can get to know each other all over again. It's been a long time.

Why were you going to court? You don't have to tell me if you don't want to. But I hope you're thinking of other ways to support yourself besides strutting your stuff in the street. I can't tell you how to live your life, but if you end up staying with me for any length of time, you've gotta stop. At least you're making progress kickin' the "monkey" off your back. You're a lot more fun to be around when you're clean and sober.

Cindy, I haven't lived with anyone in years. Hope I'm not getting in over my head. You should know beforehand how much I enjoy my privacy. I need lots of time alone. Cuddling on the couch watching TV doesn't cut it with me. I'd rather sit around watching spiders swing the air in search of prey. I even like to write poems about spiders. You probably think I'm crazy, but the older you get, the more those little things in life grow in importance. You'll see.

There you have it. If you wanna take a chance, I'm game. You'll love the apartment. The bedroom is huge. One wall is all mirrors. HMMMMM!

Oh, yeah, can you cook? Hope so. I like my meals on the table the minute I get home from work. (Just kidding.)

What your mother said about older men is true. Sounds like she was quite the woman. What about your father? Funny, we never talked about personal stuff in the ten years we've known each other.

Oh well ...

As ever,
Billy

June 16, 1996

Dear Billy,

June 29th is a done deal. I tell you, Billy, you really do come through for me. That is one quality I have always liked about you; almost makes you appear charming.

A bedroom with one wall covered in mirrors can get some men in a lot of trouble with me. You sure you can handle this? My devotion to motion has increased tenfold since I last saw you. And, no, I don't plan on pulling tricks in order to get by. From now on, I'm strictly legit.

So, curiosity kills the cat. You want to know why I'm in trouble, eh? It's actually funny, well, sort of. Maybe embarrassing is more like it. I was arrested for shoplifting again. Tampons! Can you believe it? The judge, upon seeing that my record isn't crystal clear, gave me a one-month suspended sentence. All over two boxes of plugs. Now you know my bloody secret (hahaha). Sorry it wasn't more spectacular, like a bank robbery or espionage. I don't even know why I mentioned it.

You also inquired about my father; I might as well tell you. He was cruel; a pervert and a drunk. He treated my mother quite badly. One night, eight years after I was born, he left, and never came back. My mother cried for a week, then packed our things, and we moved to Baltimore. That's how I ended up here. It's the only place I have truly known as home. Now I just want to leave all over again. Crazy, isn't it?

I need some space, as well, when I get there. I have a lot to consider about myself, my life, you, work, and things in general.

I look forward to our hotel accommodations. Hope they have a wet bar and a Jacuzzi. Wall mirrors wouldn't hurt, either. It has been a long time.

Take care, my man ...
Cindy

June 20, 1996

Cindy,

I've got us a room at the Marriott. Two nights. It'll set me back $250, but you're worth it. Maybe you can hang out at the hotel bar and make the money back for me. Again, just kidding. You know me. Don't worry, I can handle you. I'll bring my "pimp whip" along to keep you in line. Hey, what can I say? I'm a dirty old man. You love it anyway.

You refer to your mother and father in the past tense. Are they both dead? I guess it doesn't matter, or does it? Whatever, I'll drop the subject. There is no future when the present is buried in the past.

Busted for stealing tampons? Jesus Christ! I thought you were above that. I mean, why such a stupid thing as tampons? The last time you got busted for shoplifting, it was worth it. Would have been nice if you didn't get caught. I could've used that leather coat. I'm wondering, though, how are you gonna find a legitimate job with a record like yours? I don't wanna discourage you, but it is a concern, no? Something good will happen if you make it happen.

Time to get ready for another night behind the wheel. I still need $200 to cover the security deposit. Furniture is another problem. We don't have any. At least I don't. Salvation Army, here I come. I'm gonna buy a queen-size bed and some satin sheets. Big fluffy pillows. Maybe I should forget the bed and throw a mattress on the floor. They don't squeak!

No need to write back. I'll be there to pick you up. I'll drop you off at the hotel, or you can ride around with me in the cab until my shift is over. Your choice. But I better warn you ahead of time. I'm feeling like a bull in heat.

Brace yourself.

Waiting patiently,
Billy

June 24, 1996

Part Two

Billy,

I'm back in Baltimore. Sorry things didn't work out the way we planned. I know I have issues, but so do you; even though you won't admit it. Right now, I have nothing else to say. I need some serious time alone to sort things out. My post office box is still open if you care to write.

Cindy

September 1, 1996

Cindy,

What the fuck is going on? I come home from work, and you're gone. Clothes and all. No note. Nothing! Why? Just because we had a stupid argument? I never would have hit you if you didn't come at me with a knife.

The way I see it, if you're gonna stand up to me like a man, you should be able to take a punch like a man. It wasn't even a punch. A little slap. Big deal! Besides, I thought maybe it would calm you down. You always liked it when I played rough with you. Did your daddy rough you up, too? I'm sorry. That was uncalled for. But I'm pissed. I feel betrayed.

Ever since you got the job as a hostess at the "Capital Grille," you haven't been the same. The joint closes at midnight, and you were coming home when the sun comes up. Whenever I asked you about it, you put on an attitude like it was none of my business. You were probably fucking the boss, or one of those crooked politicians who hang out there.

Oh yeah, you said I have issues but won't admit it. Clue me in. I can't wait to hear your psychiatric evaluation. And thanks for leaving me with a $300 phone bill. You sure made a lot of calls to Baltimore. I thought you said you didn't have any friends down there.

Another lie.

Don't waste any nickels trying to contact me. I've already had it disconnected.

That's it! Good luck!

You're gonna need it ...

Billy

September 4, 1996
*

I feel like a big fucking sucker.

Dear Billy,

I was lost, Billy. That's the only way I can describe it. Up there in Providence with you, I knew no one, well, besides you. And the way the men at work kept looking at me, and talking about me; I just couldn't do it anymore. I couldn't be a failure to you and still look you straight in the face and smile, all the while knowing I was lying.

I tried so hard not to hook while up there. Sure, the money's much better, even than the Grille, but I promised you, and I promised myself. I couldn't keep those promises; that's why I left. I'm sorry I couldn't tell this to you face to face. I didn't mean for this to happen, Billy. I really didn't. Besides, you're better off without me. I'd just bring you down. Your writing is coming along so well, and you are staying sober, keeping up your place, and holding down a job; I'd mess everything up.

That knife incident and you slapping me, I want to forget it. You should know that I wouldn't try to hurt you if I were clear-headed and coherent. As for the comment about my father, I'd expect something foul like that out of your mouth in anger.

I'm staying with a friend of mine back in Baltimore. She lives about four blocks from my P.O. Box. I paid for that box a year in advance, so it's good. You can reach me there. I'm sorry, Billy. I really liked being up there with you. Please write.

Love,
Cindy

Sept. 7th, 1996

Cindy,

It's taken me this long to write back because I needed to cool off. Put things in perspective. I know now never to trust you again—at least not in a close relationship. Basically, you're a whore and a drug addict. And all whores and drug addicts lie. If they can't cover their lies, they avoid questions.

In your letter there was no mention of the $300 phone bill "we" have—and no mention of all the so-called friends down there you said you didn't have. Now you tell me you're living with a girlfriend. Yeah, right. I wouldn't be surprised if you were living in a fancy hotel with some kinky millionaire. I guess working at the "Capital Grille" woke you up to where the real money is.

Can't say that I blame you. It's better than going down on sleazy tomcats in some back alley for a few lousy bucks or a piece of rock. I don't know. Maybe it's the way you were built. The way you were brought up. I do know I'm tired of trying to figure it out. From now on, that's your problem—and your problem, alone. I hope you figure that out someday.

The writing was going good before you left. It's going even better now. I'm sending out poems for the first time in over a year. Like you said, I'm better off without you. I slipped and fell off the wagon for a week after you left. It took me three days to recover. That's when I finally began to see you in the light. You have a perfect body and a perfect face. Enough cosmopolitan charm when you need it to survive. You can drive a man wild in bed and crazy at the same time. Other than that, it's like you said. You're lost. I wish things could have turned out differently.

Good luck,
Billy

October 1, 1996

Dear Billy,

Lorraine, the woman I am staying with, picked my mail up today. Seems like bad luck followed me all the way from Providence to Baltimore. I'm in the hospital. Kidney infection. The first night was real bad. I'm on IV fluids and medication. They are running a bunch of tests, and I don't know when I'll be out of here.

I was lying in the hospital bed with all these machines hooked up to me, thinking how much I wished you were here. Still am. The Doctor just said that one of my tests came back abnormal. He mentioned some scan that he scheduled for later today. I guess this is what my life has come to. At least being in the hospital has kept me clean ... hopefully I'll stay that way after I get discharged.

I don't understand your anger toward me; it's almost obscene. You sound like a two-year-old throwing a tantrum. Grow up, Billy. For God's sake, I'm in the hospital, probably dying from who knows what, and you are complaining of this and that like a spoiled brat.

So I left; it happens. Life doesn't always follow the course you like. I hope you can stop pouting and come to your senses. As far as the phone bill goes, I'll send my share of the bill as soon as I'm able. I hope that's enough to satisfy you. And yes, I am glad your poetry is coming along so well.

Take care,
Cindy

Oct. 9, 1996

p.s. I am at The University of Maryland Hospital.

Dear Billy,

I haven't heard from you in quite some time, almost a month, and I am starting to worry. Did you get the $50 check I mailed to you? I am going to try and pay off that phone bill as fast as possible. As soon as I left the hospital (I was there for a week!), I started to waitress downtown in Fells Point. Business is fair; the weather, very cold. I do work on the side to help out with the bills. Nothing fancy, just companionship.

I've been staying with Lorraine but still am feeling lonely. Why haven't you contacted me? No letters or poems, nothing at all. I hope you're all right. You're not drinking again, are you?

Billy, I want you to be a part of my life in some fashion, definitely not as an enemy. You know what I mean. I am still clean; I even got my hair cut. My long reddish hair is now shoulder length.

What is holding you back from contacting me?

My address hasn't changed. Please write.

Oh, Happy Thanksgiving.

Take care,
Cindy

Nov. 20th, 1996

Dear Cindy,

The holiday shoppers remind me of ants feasting on a glazed donut. A whole colony of ants. The donut as monstrous as a shopping mall. I was just published in a broadside called Alpha Beat. First poem I've published in over a year. Anyway, that's what I've been doing with my time when not dealing with clowns and werewolves.

I'm obsessed when under the influence of the muse. The fact that I always drift back to the poem as a sort of survival technique tells me most of what I need to know about true love. Or maybe there's a big hole in my soul that only the poem can fill. And maybe it's too much to ask of any woman to understand and accept that.

As for you and me, what's left to be said? I'm not going there, you're not coming here. Besides, I'm considering a lifestyle change that I can't talk about right now. Gotta work out the particulars. The bottom line is I have to bolt from the cab business (at least on a regular basis) before my star dies away as a tiny white dwarf.

Yes, I did receive the $50 you sent. Forget the rest. It's all water washed ashore at this point. I'm still curious though about all the calls you made and never explained. I checked those numbers before having the phone disconnected. All but one made to public pay phones. Strange! Even more strange is the one not made to a public pay phone. Why would you call the police department in Baltimore? No wonder you've been evasive.

Glad you're out of the hospital and working a straight gig. At least most of the time. It's no longer any of my business what you do on the side. It never really was, I guess.

Take care,
Billy

December 10, 1996

Dear Billy,

Finally, you responded! I was worried there for a while. I thought I was going to have to come back up to Providence and bail you out of jail or worse: identify you at the morgue.

I'm assuming your Thanksgiving went well. I spent mine waitressing. We had some pretty lonely truck drivers come through, but not once did I hitch up my skirt or flash my legs. Not that I wasn't tempted, all that easy cash, but it's not them I want all over me.

I've been clean since I left the hospital. I realize that life is very precious, and I don't have all the time in the world to do what I want to. I know that love doesn't come knocking at the door every day. And that lost chances may never be found.

Thanks for lifting the phone bill debt. I'll consider it a Christmas present from you. Regarding those calls to the pay phones downtown, well, it was someone who took care of me a few years ago. We have kept in contact ever since.

The phone call involving the Baltimore Police Department is complicated, Billy. I've had what you could call 'interactions' with a Detective there. He once arrested me, and of course, we made 'arrangements' that secured my release, and consequently I didn't go to jail. Well, he saw me again, and we dated, but that was years ago, Billy. I only called to check up on him, you know, see if he was still around. He could come in handy if things go bad for me down here.

You say you have decided to make a "drastic lifestyle change." Please include me in it. I can't remember the last time I hurt like this for something. Merry Christmas, Billy.

Love,
Cindy

Dec. 18, 1996

Dear Cindy,

There is no ending without a beginning. I was thinking the other night about the first time we met all those years ago. You were walking down Dalaine Street on the West Side. As I passed by in the cab, you waved at me, and I pulled over thinking you needed a ride. You jumped in the front seat and made me an offer I couldn't say no to—especially since I had a few grand to blow from an accident case I'd recently settled. Any of this sound familiar to you?

Remember we ended up in that seedy motel out on Route 6 for a whole week? All we did was fuck and smoke dope. And when all the bills on the money tree were gone, we went our separate ways— or so we thought. Was it fate or coincidence that our paths would cross again? How is it that I became your driver, protector, confidante, occasional sex-partner, part-time pimp, and above all, a friend? The kind of friend you really enjoy having around no matter the circumstances. That's what we had, and such a friendship served us both well.

But let's face it, living together was a disaster. Yet, still you plead with me to somehow include you in my 'lifestyle change,'— which is ironic considering what this 'lifestyle change' entails. What do you want to do, get married and have babies? I'm not trying to push you away. I'm just trying to understand what's happening here. I already told you I've lost trust in you, and that I'm tired of trying to figure the whole mess out.

On the other hand, maybe I have figured it out based on something else I told you in a letter, "You're a whore and a drug addict, and all whores and drug addicts lie." Just because you've been clean for a month doesn't mean "The Monkey" is off your back. It's still on your mind. That's easy to see when the stories you come up with to explain your mysterious and erratic behavior are so full of holes they defy rhyme and reason. It's like they say—"once a junkie, always a junkie."

In one letter you told me you're 'doing a little work on the side' to help with the bills. In your last letter you told me about all the lonely truck drivers on Thanksgiving that you could have had for extra cash—then went on to say—"It's not them I want all over me."

The lesson to be learned with that one is if you're gonna lie you gotta have a good memory. And all those calls to payphones really stretch my imagination. The phone calls to the so-called

Detective sounds good on the surface. But one can only imagine what I'd find if I started digging.

The sad part about all of this is not so much the lies you tell me, and obviously others, but the lies you tell yourself. Think about that. And think about this—there is no beginning without an ending. I don't know what else to say.

Sincerely,
Billy

Christmas Day, 1996

*

Let your hair grow back.

OF SMALL THINGS   95

Dear Billy,

I'm tired of all the stories that I'm deceiving you. I don't lie to myself. Look at you, writing a boastful letter to me, all high up on your horse, calling me a whore, a liar, an addict, a cheat. Have you looked in the mirror lately? You aren't exactly a saint.

You preach from the platform "I've made a lifestyle change" and expect me to say 'okay,' 'you're the man'; 'you can treat me like garbage.' Billy, you drive a cab and write poetry that rarely gets published. And you're alone; no dog, no wife, no children, nothing but your right hand and a case of beer. Sure, living together didn't work out exactly as we planned, but now I'm alone, too.

And I try not to lash out at you, but life's frustrating as it is, and I don't claim to be the greatest woman ever. I'm an "off again, on again addict," hooker, and a poor cook. But my heart is good. And we've had so many good times together. There's still plenty of time for more.

Look, why don't you fill me in on this 'lifestyle change' and get back to me? I have some things to sort out.

Take care,
Cindy

Jan. 2, 1997

Dear Cindy,

Yeah, I've looked in the mirror lately. Have you? Listen, I don't wanna get us into a "husband and wife" shouting match, or a star-crossed "lovers' quarrel." We're not married, and we're not really lovers. I don't know what we are, or that it even matters anymore. Just forget everything I said. But before you forget, know that I wasn't preaching. I had (still do) serious reservations about a lot of things you've said in the past six/seven months. Why should I try and maintain a relationship with anyone under such a cloud of doubt? Would you? I know you'll say I'm being paranoid and all that, and maybe you're right. But that's the way it is with me right now.

    That's right. I am alone. No wife. No children. Not even a dog. By the looks of things, you're in the same boat. At least I have poetry along for the ride. And you're wrong about it never getting published. It hasn't been in a long time, but I'm making a comeback. The following was recently accepted in a journal called BARBARIC YAWP. It's called "Wages of Love."

> Love like yours, my love—
> Stranger than truth or fiction,
> Is twice the price of knee-deep danger—
> A hindrance in my struggle to survive.
> The path you clear these days is narrow—
> Not much room for two to travel.
> My regrets yet are few—
> As are the weeds in Eden.
> Profit being in the loss.

Can you dig it? I can't talk about the 'other thing' in a letter or on the telephone. It might be better if I don't tell you. You might salivate to death. I had to laugh when you said I have nothing but my right hand and a case of beer to keep me company. There are plenty of others out there to "lend me a hand" when I need it. And I need it now, so I gotta go.

Billy

January 10, 1997

Billy,

I'm tired of playing this cat and mouse game with you. It's obvious by the tone of your recent letters (especially the last one) that you consider our relationship to be in the past tense. The last line of your poem says it all: "Profit being in the loss."

Have it your way.

Hope you found another hand to take the place of your own. I know the feeling. I need a "prick" to take your place. And I need it now so I have to go.

Cindy

January 16, 1997

Dear Crazy Cindy,

It doesn't matter how an accident happens, or whose fault it is. All that matters is that it happened. If one or more survive this accident without serious injury there is only one option open to them. Pick up the pieces and move on. Drive away or get a new piece—as in piece of ...

The mechanic who works on my brain isn't sure he can fully repair the damage done. He sent me to a head doctor who suggested the problem is not my brain, but instead in the unexamined "junkyard of my soul" where many replacement parts can be found. My heart loathes me to go there. They were abandoned years ago. An intensive search would be the end of me. And what would I do with these replacement parts? The pieces that have held me together since I can remember have always kept me afloat—especially when my feet were not on the ground. So this is what it's come to—Oh, what a wreck is me/all bent and broke/bereft of even bluffer. That's it!

No more 'bluffing around' in search of what isn't there, or what I think should or shouldn't be there. It's like the old saying goes—"It is what it is." Such is my perception of reality. And yes, I'm aware that senses can be deceiving. I don't have time enough to care about these complexities and contradictions anymore.

I want to see you. I'll go there. If you need money to hide us away for a few days, let me know, and I'll send Western Union. I will explain everything when we meet. Oh yeah, I'll be looking forward to my birthday present.

Seriously,

And with affection,
Billy

January 20, 1997

Dear Billy,

I'm not sure I like your idea. Don't get me wrong; I wouldn't mind seeing you again, but you sound like you have some sort of hidden agenda on your mind. All that talk about comparing our relationship to an accident confuses me. Not that I don't agree up to a point, but all that other stuff you bring up. The mechanic who works on your brain? The unexamined 'junkyard of your soul' where your heart loathes going? Why are you speaking in riddles?

    You were always paranoid, but now I think you've gone off the deep-end. Either that or you were drunk. Probably drunk and stoned. I thought you gave all that stuff up? What did you get yourself into, Billy? You worry me.

    Come on down to Baltimore. You'll get your chance; one chance. And I want to know what's going on in plain English. I hope you know what you're doing. Just let me know when you're coming so I can plan a few days off from work. I have some money stashed and can rent us a place to stay.

    Maybe we can put those pieces back together again.

Take care,
Cindy

P.S. Should I pack heels *and* running shoes?

January 26, 1997

Dear Cindy,

Sorry I got you all confused in my last letter. You know how I get
when I fall into that 'poetic state of mind.' I thought. Never mind
what I thought. It doesn't matter. I can be there a week from today.
I'll be driving a rental car.

As soon as you get this write back letting me know when and
where to meet you. If you can't pull it off for next weekend, that's
O.K. For the time being, I'm flexible. Don't worry; I don't have an
agenda against you. You won't need running shoes. I already told
you my 'new thing' would make you salivate. At least I think it
will—unless you've suddenly turned into a saint.

Can't wait ...

As always,
Billy

February 1, 1997

Dear Billy,

Next week is good for me; say Friday around 7 p.m. Meet me downtown at the Inner Harbor, outside of Pier One.

I'll book a hotel for one week. When you get here, we'll figure out where to stay if we need more time.

I'll be wearing that little black dress you gave me a while back.

Take care,
Cindy

Feb. 4th, 1997

Billy,

What's going on?

Here I am alone on a Saturday night. I want to be mad at you, but I'm worried. It isn't like you not to show up when you say you are.

Cindy

February 13, 1997

Dear Cindy,

I've got a problem. The night before I was supposed to leave for Baltimore, I got arrested. I was arraigned this morning and bail has been set at $25,000 with 10% security. I have a bail bondsman, but as you know he wants that 10% before securing my release. I would have had the money, but the police confiscated it as evidence against me.

I can't provide you with any details right now but promise to tell you everything if and when I get out of here. If you can, send money to Western Union (payable to Angelo Santoro) at 777 River Street, New Bedford, Massachusetts, 02907. I'm in the New Bedford House of Correction (Intake Center). The address is 312 County Street, 02907 (Unit B). My prisoner ID # is 6484.

I could use a good lawyer but will probably be forced to accept the court-appointed public defender they assigned to my case. One last thing, Western Union probably takes a 10% processing fee ($250), and I'll need a few bucks for myself to get going again. $3,000 is the bottom line.

Sorry to put this all on your shoulders, but I don't have anyone else to go to for help. If you decide not to do anything, or can't do anything, I'll understand.

Love,
Billy

February 15, 1997

Dear Billy,

You must really be hurting in jail to ask me for $3,000. That's a lot, Billy, a whole lot. What have you gotten yourself into this time? But yes, of course, I will wire the money. You owe me big time for this one.

I can't do it until tomorrow, though. I have some prior obligations to attend to that I can't get out of. Billy, when are we going to get our lives back together? I mean, we keep messing up ...

I need to make some money and fast. Being with you isn't cheap, but the love is good when it's good. Hope you stay safe in there.

Love,
Cindy

February 17, 1997

Dear Cindy,

I just got out today. Not sure of my next move. No money and the rent will soon be due. The public defender claims that the taxi commission can't suspend my license until/and if I'm convicted as charged. I'll know in a few days.

O.K., time to come clean. Since last Christmas, I've been driving for an escort service. I got the job from a chick named Mimi that I knew from Fantasy Bar years ago. We met by chance, and after one night working for her, I earned double than my taxi job in the same amount of time.

The risks of this job kept me from telling you about it. I didn't think I was breaking any laws, either. The girls were into prostitution and carrying dope. You know how paranoid I used to be about carrying drugs around in the cab, but damn that easy money.

The night I got arrested, I had taken one of the girls to a suburb outside of Boston to meet with a client. The minute we pulled up to this client's address, cops were all over us. I have only one idea why.

It had to be a set-up. She had warrants and an 'ounce' of coke in her purse. We were both charged. I was also in violation of some law called the Mann Act. It's all so crazy and confusing.

The bottom line is that now I face some serious jail time, if convicted. The only good news is that all my prior felonies were expunged years ago, before I got my license to drive cab.

The lawyer thinks I can beat the drug and harboring charges since the drugs were found on her person—and how was I to know she was wanted on all those old warrants? The transporting across state lines for immoral purposes is where I might be screwed. I can't say we were out on a date because I don't even know her real name.

I could say I was the client. That would leave me with the misdemeanor charge of solicitation. But how do I explain the car being registered to a business with its office in a suite on the top floor of the Biltmore Hotel? I just don't know. I'll wait and see what the lawyer says. We go for pre-trial motions on March 28th.

I can't think of anything else to say right now—except thanks. One way or another, I'll make it up to you. You're the only one in my life I can count on. If you have a phone number I can reach you at, let me know. I really wanna hear your voice. Just be careful what you say on the phone. And don't forget to throw out all our correspondence. You never know who's listening or looking for any secrets you might have.

Write me as soon as you can.
Billy

February 23, 1997

Dear Billy,

When things are good, they're good. When they're bad, well, they're bad. So here's my only secret we have to worry about: yesterday, I got a ticket for prostitution. Jails are so overcrowded, they give out tickets with court dates so I lucked out and skipped the typical booking and bail hearing. However, I have to show up for court on March 15th—so close to yours.

I talked with Lorraine about you, about me, about how we can't meet up with each other. We're a mess, Billy. But for now, we are both out of jail. What are you going to do? I have a friend, he's a cop actually. Well, he has helped me before. I tried to reach him earlier and had to leave a message. He requires favors in return, but I don't have a better idea for me.

So you've been driving call girls around town, eh? I should've known. You're a sucker when they flash all that money in your face. The hooker you picked up really messed you up; such a stupid trick.

I'm not mad at you anymore. Both of us are broke—I could hitch a ride up to Providence? No. Better not. I don't want to risk getting busted up there, as well. Besides, your public defender sounds like he knows what he's doing. We've both been through much worse. We'll survive this one way or another.

Ever get the feeling you just 'want to go home'? Oh, to be young again. I don't have a phone anymore. The bill was pretty high, so I couldn't afford it. They shut it off a few days ago. Oh, and stop being so paranoid. You have always been a 'worrier.'

Write me soon. I don't want to waste valuable time.

Love,
Cindy

February 26th, 1997

Dear Cindy,

I'm sorry. You were doing so well, and I forced you back into the street to bail me out of a jam. Hopefully, that cop can help you out again. Do what you have to do. I don't mean to sound insensitive, but there's nothing I can do.

The public defender was wrong. The taxi commission suspended my license to drive a cab pending the outcome of my case. I can't drive for the escort service and the landlord wants the rent. I contacted Mimi, and she hooked me up with the guy who owns the Fantasy Bar. They have rooms upstairs, and he offered me a job as a desk clerk at night. I can live in one of the rooms for $25 a day or $160 a week. I had to take the job. What else could I do? I guess I'll be renting a room there, as well. The job doesn't pay much, but at least I'll have a roof over my head, and I won't go hungry. That's about it.

I met Mimi a few years ago while she was a dancer at the high-end strip joints up and down the coast. She did 'expensive' tricks on the side, which led her to start an escort service. She lives at the upscale Biltmore. She claims no illegal knowledge of the trick I was transporting. She doesn't ask and doesn't tell. She's a smart broad.

Not much else to say. Hope that woman, Lorraine, is a good friend of yours so you won't have to worry about a place to stay.

Waiting patiently ...
Billy

March 3, 1997

Dear Billy,

The cop I know talked to the prosecuting attorney on my behalf. The prosecutor talked with my public defender, and it looks like I'll just get probation if I plead nolo. I'll take that, but now I owe the cop a favor. He'll let me know; whatever that means.

Since you finally asked, Lorraine is my younger sister. I never brought her up before because it's not an easy issue to talk about. My father never preyed on her like he did me, and I've always held a silent grudge. Sometimes I wish her away. But I'm working on that issue. She's always been good to me.

I can't believe they suspended your license. And now you're a desk clerk, too! I'd love to see that. Actually, being a desk clerk may give you time to write when business is slow. Rick's Fantasy Bar, eh? Be careful with your money on pleasure spending. I don't need you in any more trouble. Our lives are on the edge of destruction already. As for Mimi, let it be. She sounds deceitful. I think she knew more about the incident than she's admitted.

I am unable to help you financially right now, sorry. Do you have any family that can help? I don't recall you ever mentioning relatives.

After all this is over, let's go home together. I don't mean make babies, attend barbeques and cocktail parties. Let's live a life worth living, and do it together. Do you like baseball?

Take care and be safe.

Love,
Cindy

March 8, 1997

Dear Cindy,

You could have told me that Lorraine was your sister. It wouldn't have changed anything between us. But it does make me wonder how many more secrets you have. I can only imagine what that cop friend of yours wants in return for the so-called favor he did for you.

Well, the job is boring, and the 'cast of characters' living here are not exactly model citizens. But in fairness, neither am I, when you think about it. Do you still have your job at the restaurant? You can't work the street anymore, that's for sure. Maybe all that's happening in our lives right now is a blessing in disguise. In any case, don't worry about me. I'll get by.

The girl I got busted with is in jail as a probation violator. Between the old warrants and the new charges against her, she'll end up doing some serious time. The good news is that in her statement to the police she told them that the drugs belong to her, and that I knew nothing of the old warrants out for her arrest.

You asked me about my family. My father died when I was seventeen. I left home a year later and never returned—not even for the funerals of three siblings. My mother is still alive, but we haven't talked in years. I'm not even sure where she lives. There's more to the story, but I'm sort of in a hurry right now. I have to vacuum and clean the dressing room for the dancers. Can you believe that? Go ahead and laugh if you want. I think it's kinda funny.

O.K.! Good luck in court.

As always,
Billy

March 11, 1997

Yeah, I like baseball.

Dear Billy,

Deepest sympathies regarding your three siblings; I never knew. I'm glad you have rebounded from all of it.

I was quite scared at court, but all went well. Probation with a suspended sentence is a good deal for me. I've faced worse.

The cop who gave me the 'edge' wanted 'in' on some names for his own personal business. What a freak! I gave up a few older contacts as they were ignorant to me when I worked with them. Paybacks. I told him from the beginning that I was 'attached' but had a few ideas that I thought he would like.

Lorraine being my sister compared to drugged-out Cindy is embarrassing, so I usually leave that association out. In fact, I think you are the first person I've disclosed this to.

How is your poetry coming along? Who got you started? I mean, you said your family wasn't around? You know, some days I wonder what would've happened had I met you years ago. How would things have turned out? Or not turned out?

Our paths came together for a reason—I don't believe in accidents or coincidence. I hope you can pull away from your past just like I hope to pull away from mine.

This arrest and sentence has me motivated. Thanks for wishing me well at court. The support helped.

I'm still clean and sober. I am also saving some money for us once we decide exactly what we are doing. Hope you can and are doing the same.

Let me know what's going on, besides sweeping floors, which I admit was a pretty funny image. I like hard workers. I like you. Keep in touch.

Love,
Cindy

March 20, 1997

Cindy,

Finally saw the lawyer today. I'm definitely caught in the middle of some stupid 'sting operation' designed to bust the interstate 'flesh trade' based here in Providence. The cops have taped recordings of all conversations between client and girl they arrested. Client also a cop who was working undercover.

They're willing to drop the drug and harboring charges against me, but won't budge on the charge of transporting for immoral purposes, unless I lead them closer to the top. How can I do that without implicating Mimi? The bottom line is that if I work with them, I go free. But how free will I be if I'm working for the cops?

And how can I turn against Mimi who never did me any harm? Not to mention the likely fact that her business is also the business of others who would think nothing of drilling a hole in my head. If I don't play their game and go to trial, I could get up to two years with eighteen months to serve if I lose. And how can I win?

What can I do or say to convince a jury I'm innocent when I'm really not? I'd never remember all the lies I'd have to tell to get over on them. So, I'm fucking stuck here with three days to make a decision.

Maybe I should just plead guilty and get it over with. Nothing left to say about this mess I'm in. No sense writing back until you hear from me again.

Thanks for the nice letter. Glad everything went well for you in court. And good to know you're clean and sober. I'm rooting for you. Fuck that cop over in Baltimore. You don't need him as long as you stay on the right side of the road.

Miss you much ...
Billy

March 23, 1997

Dear Cindy,

Unless a miracle happens, I won't be around for a while.

The girl I got busted with went to court today and agreed to plead nolo to all charges. They reduced the charges of violating the Mann Act to "conspiracy to do so." The person on the other end of those taped conversations is most likely a confidential informant who the cops don't wanna expose.

The girl won't be sentenced for a few months. If she's talking to cops hoping for light time, she'll no doubt implicate me. I'm fucked.

The lawyer says the DA has to reduce the charges against me to conspiracy, as well. But they'll still recommend to the judge that I serve six months of a one-year sentence. In the end, it's up to the judge. My unwillingness to cooperate with the cops won't help my case.

There's nothing much left to say. If you don't hear back from me in a few days, it means I'm gone. I'll let you know my new address ASAP.

Love,
Billy

March 24, 1997

Part Three

Dear Cindy,

I got what the DA recommended—a year with six months suspended and six to serve. I'm at the Wyatt Detention Center in Walpole, MA. Write me when you can. You know the rules.

Billy

April 5, 1997

Wyatt Detention Center
2130 Old Mill Road
Walpole, MA 02788

*
My ID # is 2135

Dear Billy,

Hi hon. Six months, eh? I hope you are all right.

I have my work cut out for me. I can send letters, money orders, and one or two 'care packages,' but I can't afford to visit right now. I need to make money and fast.

Well, at least you don't have to serve the full year. It could be worse for us, Billy. I'm confident you'll do fine there. I heard Wyatt isn't really a bad place—but not as nice as Martha Stewart's Camp Cupcake (hahaha).

I'll send a money order in a few days. I'll also send you a sexy photo, if I can come up with one.

Meanwhile, take care, and keep in touch.

Love,
Cindy

April 10, 1997

Dear Cindy,

Thanks for the letter, and your concern. I'll be all right. I know how to mind my own business. Sexy photos? Don't make them too sexy. Having pictures of you to stare at might make my time harder —no pun intended. Then again, I may never get to even see them if the staff decides to read my mail.

I'm just about processed and ready to start working in the library. The advantage to that is I get a little extra time to use the typewriter and read, as well. I'll be making about 80 cents a day. Imagine that. Speaking of money; if you can send me $20, I'd appreciate it. I need stamps and writing materials in a bad way. Sorry to even ask, but ...

Well, we have six months to talk about the future. The future is kind of scary. I'm going to be 62 when I get out of here. No money, no job, no place to go. I don't even qualify to collect social security. Are you sure you wanna stay involved with me? You're still young. You have plenty of game left. I just don't want you to feel like I'm your responsibility.

Time for lunch. Bologna sandwiches and tomato soup. Coffee milk. Haven't had that in years. Tapioca pudding for dessert. I remember how my mother made that for me all the time when I was just a kid. O.K.!

Looking forward ...
Billy

April 17, 1997

Dear Billy,

Glad you're okay. I wouldn't expect you not to be, but still ... That job working in the library sounds like the old you. Maybe you can send me a poem or two? Come to think of it, I haven't picked up a book in years. These last few years have really flown by.

New things are happening on my end of town. I got a part-time job at a bar my friend visits a lot. He also knows the owner and got me an interview. It went well, so I start in four days.

I'll send you a money order in an envelope by itself. My friend told me that's how it's done. He knows a lot about these things, so that helps. Oh, a "care package" will have to wait until I have one or two paychecks under me. I'm still establishing myself. Same address, but need the fillings. Also need more stamps to keep writing!

Bologna does sound bad and so does the tomato soup, too. I'd stick with the pudding. My Mother made the greatest pancakes—no pudding; lucky you. But my Mom's pancakes were made from 'scratch.' She'd say, "I woke up earlier than usual just to make you my special pancakes." They were the best, and we were extra nice to her all day long. Turns out her pancakes were nothing but store-bought mix added with water. I learned a lot from that woman.

We got caught up in the mix, didn't we, Billy? I liked it way back when daisies took my attention away. Well, on to worrying about everything.

Take care—oh, the photo! No luck yet.

Sorry. Be good.

Cindy

April 25, 1997

Dear Cindy,

I like working in the library. I manage to squeeze in a few hours of my own when not classifying and arranging books. I'm reading a lot, and writing on the typewriter, mostly haiku. I don't have time to explain what that is right now, but it's fun. Go to the library (ha ha) and read all about it.

Wish you could come here—again, no pun intended. Don't forget that picture. I'm also learning how to use a computer. Amazing! You can actually send instant messages electronically. They call it e-mail. Big Walter, the other librarian, says computers are the wave of the future.

Good that your friend helped you find a job. It's helpful to have friends. Whatever. Be careful. Not that your friend will take advantage of you—which is sometimes the downside of friendship—but sometimes when you give people lots of space, they take it. Don't know if that's an original statement (maybe I heard or read it somewhere), but it's true. Think about it.

Speaking of care packages, I can't write again until I can buy stamps at the commissary. And I'm not taking any free cigarettes from anyone or else I'll be wearing "punk pants" to bed for some horny gorilla.

Mom's pancakes sound yummy. Maybe it's time you should learn to cook like her. Ya gotta take care of your man, right? Don't take that seriously. By the way, I asked once, but you never gave me an answer. Is your mother still alive—your father?

Yeah, we got mixed up all right. But we have only ourselves to blame. It's not like we didn't have choices in our lives. That's not important, though, anymore. It's the choices we make from this point on that matter most.

With love and affection,
Billy

May 3, 1997

Dear Billy,

I'm glad you have free time in the library. Computers, typewriters, they all sound too high tech for me. I'll stick to letter writing with my little red pen.

I'm looking for an apartment, or will be soon. I went to a yard sale the other day and found a desk for ten bucks, bargained down to five. Now you'll have a place to write your haiku. I also found a dining room table. I paid a little more than I can afford right now, but we need it. Lorraine is letting me store everything at her place for now. We're getting along O.K., but I sense it's time for us to go our separate ways soon.

Work is going as expected. My co-workers have a side business and offered me an opportunity to take part. The money is good. Without it, I couldn't afford to get us up once you get out. The only problem is "my friend." He hangs out there a lot and is really beginning to annoy me. He expects these "little favors" for helping me out. I can't say I didn't expect it. And I can't exactly say no. At least not right now. I hope you understand.

You asked about my mother and father. I know you asked before, but I blew it off. It's not my favorite subject. My mother passed away in 1985. She was only 49. I moved to Providence shortly after that.

My father, like I said before, left when I was eight years old. I haven't had any contact with him since. I probably wouldn't know him if I passed him on the street. He's dead for all I know, or care.

Have to get ready for work now. Hope you like the picture. I hope they let you keep it. And I hope you got the money order I sent.

Write soon.

Cindy

May 10, 1997

Dear Cindy,

Thanks for the money you sent. I bought envelopes and stamps. Lots of chocolate bars, too. They remind me of you—sweet and delicious.

Good that you're looking for an apartment. But don't forget I still have a six-month suspended sentence to serve when I get out of here. And I need permission to move there during that time. The other thing is that I'm not sure I want to live in Baltimore. At least that's the way I'm thinking right now. I have five months ahead of me in this place. Maybe I'll change my mind—or you will.

I don't think I'd like your friend. It bothers me that you have to do what you do. I feel like it's my fault. Hopefully, I can make it up to you someday. I'm wondering, did he take the picture of you? It's pretty hot stuff. If he did, I'm jealous, but what can I say. Yes, the staff allowed me to keep it.

I let Big Walter take it back to his cell last night. He said he had a good time. It's my turn tonight. The young kid in the cell next to me wants to spend a night with you, too. He even offered me a few bucks. I might take him up on it if I get desperate. Hope you don't feel like I'm invading your privacy. Ya gotta do what ya gotta do in here to get by. I'd ask you to send more but then the whole damn prison population would be in heat.

I won't ask about your mother and father anymore. Best to put the past to bed and take care of the future.

Here's a haiku:

Blue Jays in the morning mist
Hopping from branch to limb.
That nut-cracking sound.

———————————

Almost time for lunch. Tonight is movie night. "Dirty Harry" is the feature, starring Clint Eastwood.

I miss you,
Billy

May 15, 1997

Dear Billy,

I don't mind the 'photo connection.' I'm not flattered that prisoners dig me. The really good men aren't often prisoners (no offense), but who am I to talk, right? We're a pretty unique pair, the two of us. I like it. I don't like that you're considering living somewhere else; but five months in prison can change that. In the meantime, I'll keep your desk clean.

That 'haiku' you sent me is so 'here and now.' I really enjoyed it. My photo should pay for more paper and pens. I'd like to read more. Not from the library, I mean from you. Please.

I'm sorry 'my friend' has caused you grief. He causes me grief, too. I need my probation to proceed flawlessly. He can help with that.

Billy, I want to settle down. When you get out, I can quit this job and do strictly waitressing. Baltimore has always been home to me, but if you asked me to leave with you, I would.

Enjoy your library time.

Love,
Cindy.

May 22, 1997

Dear Cindy,

Can't believe I've been here two months already. I can do the rest of the time standing on my head. I saw the staff counselor today. She's recommending me for a transfer to medium security. If all goes right, I'll be there in a few weeks. No later than July 1st. By then, I'll be half-way home. If I do good there, I get to spend the last two months of my sentence in minimum. In minimum, you can have your own P.O. Box, if the counselor approves it. Then you can write and say what you want without worrying that someone else will read it.

I thought you'd be flattered that the other inmates liked your picture so much. That kid I told you about in the cell next to me has it now. I gave it up for a carton of cigarettes. Send more if it's not a problem. Big Walter said he'd buy me a book of stamps for one. And I need stamps since I've begun sending out poetry submissions.

I found a copy of the "Writer's Market" in the library and it's been a big help. I sent some haiku to one publisher, and because I'm in here, he mailed me a sample copy for free. Don't know if he accepted any of them yet. I'm also reading more than ever.

Just finished a biography of the writer, F. Scott Fitzgerald. Ever hear of him? The man was not only a great writer, but a crazy drunk, as well. Maybe when I get out, I can find a job in a library. What a switch that would be.

I'm not worried about your friend. But how is he gonna react if I ever showed up on the scene? I don't need any trouble.

I know you want to settle down. So do I. God knows it's about time. I'm just not sure under what circumstances we can make it work. By that I mean location.

Maybe I should consider getting out of Providence, for obvious reasons.

O.K., gotta get back to work. I'll send some more poems the next time around.

Love,
Billy

June 1, 1997 (It just occurred to me that my first day here was April Fool's Day.)

Dear Billy,

I've enclosed a few more pictures of me from last year. I don't own a digital camera—can't figure out how to work those things. I'm technologically-impaired. But these should do the trick (pun almost intended).

I hope you get that transfer. I like that P.O. Box situation. It feels weird knowing you're not the only one reading these letters; sort of like losing your virginity in front of people.

Work is good, but I cut back my hours so I could pick up a midnight shift at a Tavern, waitressing. I want a chance, too. I work many hours, but it's for us, and that keeps me going.

I'm so happy that you've found interest in something positive: writing. And possibly working in a library? Jail is changing you, or maybe you are just fed up, eh? Either reason, I like this new you. Will you like the 'me' out here that I'm becoming?

Four months to go—I hope we can find a life together when the time arrives. For now, I'm still waiting.

Love,
Cindy.

June 8, 1997

Dear Cindy,

You haven't aged a bit in these photos. The guys are having a bidding war over them. I'm trading for stamps, pens, paper, envelopes, but am still hurting for cigarettes.

My counselor filed for the transfer today. I'll know something these next two weeks. I have no tickets, and my boss at the library wrote an excellent work ethic report for the Board.

When I'm not working on my poetry, I think of us and our future. I feel things need to change, like jobs, how we communicate, where we live. Also, do I like the 'old us' or the 'new us'? And for me, do I want any of my past, including you, following me out of these locked doors?

Sure, sunsets are lonely. But for now, I can't even see them. There's still much to consider.

That midnight tavern shift sounds dangerous. Well, you know what you're doing.

Be good. Please send some smokes soon.

Billy

June 16, 1997

Dear Billy,

Thanks for the compliment. Sorry about the cigarettes; my money had more bills to cover than I had for cigarettes. I mailed out a box mid-week. Thanks for the reminder.

I hope you get the transfer. You're coping well in jail, as it is. You've surprised me. Otherwise, I'd be upset over this whole situation. I'm feeling pretty good out here, sober and working.

I've liked you a long time. But my life has never thrived when I'm with you in a positive way. And that doesn't sound good for us as a couple. But I want to be with you again. To give it one last go.

I know my 'friend' has to go away. And I'm working on that issue now. He'll be gone by the time you're out, definitely.

I have to go work at the Tavern now. Mailbox is on the way. The Tavern has to go, too. For now, I need the money.

Hopefully, here comes Medium Security.

Looking forward to hearing from you.

Cindy

June 23, 1997

Dear Cindy,

Thanks for the smokes. I got transferred to Medium Security yesterday. Two months here should fly by. Then one more month in Minimum.

Right now, I'm working in an extension of the prison's main library. It enables me to have more freedom, access to more books. Commissary has better selections, as well. If you can send me a $30 money order, I can purchase a typewriter. Call it an "early release present."

That job at the Tavern doesn't sound good. I'll pay you back for all of this. I'm not saying we'll be together—just that I pay my debts.

Writing is what I want to do while driving cab. You'd be number two in my life to writing—just how it is. I don't need or want much. As I've said before, I need my own space and my own personal time. I don't like being bothered when I write; I'm in my element. Can you live with someone like that? Do you want to?

I really like you. Sex will still be good, but what can I say? I'm too old to live so recklessly and wild. Time to slow down, watch the insects crawl, the grass grow, leaves change to brown.

Your thoughts?

Write back soon,
Billy

July 3, 1997

Dear Billy,

I'm glad you got the transfer. You're half-way home and in better company. Congrats.

I sent the money order for the typewriter. I can't do much else. I'm strapped for money. I'm already overworking myself. It's driving me nuts—no time off to relax, to go out with friends, etc. There's got to be something different.

There won't be any money for a while. I have to stop; pay attention to my needs. It's getting to be too much on me. Why can't you be wild anymore? Age? I never thought I'd hear that out of your mouth.

I'm going to stay in Baltimore—my family's rooted here. I know this city well. I know I said I'd change locations for you, but I don't want to start completely from scratch. I understand the ramifications that could occur because of this change of heart. I'll write soon—unless you write first. I have things to do now.

Take care,
Congrats again.

Cindy

July 18, 1997

Billy,

I wanted to write first. The job at the Tavern went bad. I made it out with my last check and myself intact. Men from up North cleaned house. All I had were suspicions.

So I am staying out of things for now. I don't seem to make the best job decisions. I am more of an opportunist.

You have close to one month left in Medium? I hope it truly is going by fast. Trouble has been following me everywhere lately— except to you.

I know my lifestyle is not how you want to live. I want your lifestyle of being in jail to be different. We both have things going against us. I don't want to live like this, and I'm sure you don't, either. My box is secure. You can still write me.

I miss the 'old us.' I know I'm failing you. I'm sorry.

Cindy

July 23, 1997

Cindy,

Your troubles are more than I need—now, and when I'm released. We can't go back to the "old us."

What are you doing? Drugs? I can't think of any other explanation. I work every day in here: Monday through Friday. On weekends, I do my poetry research. I stay where I should, do as I'm told, stay away from trouble and keep busy legally.

I know I shouldn't expect you to change overnight—but that's what I expect of myself. You don't fit my standards anymore; no sugar coating, honey. You practically blew it.

It's infuriating that you're risking our relationship over a job. You should never have put yourself into that situation again. If you are truly as sorry as your letter said, give me one good reason we should be together after my release.

You have to send the next letter to Minimum. Medium is overcrowded, and I don't present a flight risk or fight risk. I have accumulated some 'good time,' so I have about 30 to 45 more days until my release. Cindy, I don't know if we are ever going to fix each other together.

I'm waiting,
Billy

July 29, 1997

Dear Billy,

After your release, the sun will be beautiful, the weather warm. Lorraine will drive me up to get you, and we'll all leave together. You and I will finish our probations together. You will while working at the local library. I will while working at the Bed and Breakfast.

We'll both support each other's sobriety—take long walks by ourselves. You'll have as much alone time as you need. And you'll have your new typewriter and desk to use.

I'll learn how to cook from those television shows like Martha Stewart. Maybe we'll take up fishing or catch some ball games.

We'll share in the arts as I listen to your poems and learn how to draw. Enjoy some concerts. I'll channel my wildness toward something positive like work or exercise (or sex).

Billy, any and all of these are good reasons you should give me that one final chance; a chance at one more life together.

Love,
Cindy

*I love using a P.O. Box.

August 10, 1997

Dear Cindy,

Your 'dream' is nice, but this is reality. All you wrote are little girl fantasies. Flights of the imagination—almost a work of prose. And for that last one, I congratulate you. For the rest, I remain disappointed.

I wanted something concrete, definitive, and I just can't get that from you. I remember all those phone calls you made, those 'all nighters' without me, the knife argument, your hooking, and lastly, lies, drug use, and that cop affair.

Sure your body rocks; sex is excellent, intentions good. Results? Not what I want now. Not up to par with my new standards. See, in jail, I've had a lot of time to think about my future. If I'm to have one, I can't succumb to this again.

My projected release date is September 15th (this year), I still work within the library extension, write and submit poetry, haiku, still do what I gotta do. Nothing jeopardizing my future.

That's the difference between us now: I'm looking forward realistically. You're looking back at the 'old us,' only for the future. That can't happen, Cindy.

Right now, I want to hear, realistically, how you and I can live together.

Still waiting ...
Billy

August 19, 1997

Dear Billy,

Realities are born from dreams. You dreamt of writing and publishing poetry—and now you have this reality.

You once wrote "There is no beginning without an end," and I was thinking about it today, rolling it over in my head: this has to end. We have to end our relationship if either of us is to have a beginning. Who told you that garbage?!

Your riddles are like quote books nobody reads—but then pulls out when they want to sound smart. Billy, jail messed you up—made you silly. Not wise.

Bad actions by bad people get justice, but you have been ridiculing me for no reason whatsoever. You call me names, tell me how to live—you lack compassion.

You think you're in church versus jail. I'm the one who's free.

You may have to lasso somebody else with your foul mouth. There are other fish in the sea; that, I know, is always true for me.

Cindy

August 26, 1997

Dear Cindy,

Soon I'll be out of here. I won't be moving to Baltimore. In Providence, I'll carry out the remainder of my suspended sentence. I have to stay focused to have my freedom without conditions.

You're a liability to me, Cindy. Just like Mimi will be if I go back to that part of town. I've found that women get me in way too much trouble to keep. Once in a while is O.K., but nothing long-term. I don't think I'm in church, rather a stage of life that's between two times.

I have another chance to live my life, and I'm going to take it. My life is my own. I live it my way. I don't use string or bread-crumbs; my trail may grow cold.

Cindy, for once, you're right. I should lasso someone else. Like you said, 'There are many fish in the sea.'

Have a good life, Cindy. The ride's over.

Billy

September 10th, 1997

Dear Billy,

Amongst the vast cities of the world, know that if you pass me by, feel free to smile. You introduced me to many things, and I thank you for that.

I don't follow breadcrumbs or string; I follow my heart.

I'm off in another direction now, toward purple mountains, orange clay—sand that shines for miles.

And you're wrong, Billy; the ride is only beginning.

Cindy

September 15th, 1997

under a

bridge

Stephanie Hiteshew

Under
a Bridge

Stephanie Hiteshew

Claim

Siren wails
come closer to the city
than cleanliness.
Under a bridge,
pin-eyed,
you narrowly smile.
I hold your hand
coated in bruises,
breathing in a fog
you'd see
over a pier at night.
I sigh and say prayers.
The truth
I can't turn toward
(or away).
I leave you
under blankets.
Soul free
to lay its claim.

One Second

Only have
one chance.

Clouds sour
the balmy sun.

Over you go.

One second
a brand new
tomorrow.

No fence too
high.
No door
locked tight
enough.

Over the Road

It's a young day.
The sun rises
over the road.
I put on my shoes,
roll up my blanket.
These glorious mornings
without distraction,
the sun hitting the sky
as I hit the road.

Magic

Livin' the way
we did,
like magic
hard-in-the-making.
How much water
can you wring
from a sponge?
How much livin'
can you do
before you start
dying?

Principles of Escape

Although the door was unlocked,
I didn't leave.
The doctor
never understood that.
At the moment,
he was discreetly concerned.
I guess he thought
I didn't notice
the other person leave
without using a key.

I did, and later acknowledged
that fact
but declined to comment
on why I didn't escape;
the way you do when asked
if you stole your parents' car
or cheated on your calculus test.

But between you and me,
an escape must be something spectacular.
How daring is it to run out an unlocked door?

Surrender

The ache
of a million
nods lost—
pain like
you'll surrender
to any random
bullet.

STEPHANIE HITESHEW

Home

Went to the bank,
unfortunately,
no one robbed it.
Over to the gas station
where nothing caught fire.
Down to the lake
and found
no one drowning.
Came home
to an empty house
wanting entertainment.

More

Let me know
when your moment
is over,
that initial high
when dope climbs
through your system,
rushes into your head
before relaxing,
so I can tell you
I have more.

Studio

In our studio apartment
they gave us a bed
and fan,
two second-story
windows with a view
of the liquor store
and two guys under
arrest.

Style

Bring on
the dirt roads,
the crumbling
bridges over narrow
creeks.
The "kick it all
in my face,
throw the world
at my fingertips," style.
I'm taking every road
I find—
even the ones
I have to make.

STEPHANIE HITESHEW

The World

For the road,
it was two
more feet
pounding.
For me,
it was
taking on
the world.

Good to Be Home

We walk the empty
parking lots,
the abandoned
train tracks,
green concrete school-
yards,
the clouds following
without wind.
We make our way
to the bend of a road.
So good to be home.
So good.

Fence

The fence wasn't built
to keep you safe
but to keep us safe.
Us: the streakers,
manics, schizophrenics.
You: the closed-door
drunks, tax-evaders,
and cheaters.
Main difference:
we were caught.
Besides, we learned
long ago
how to climb that fence.

Waited

Out of the wind.
Out of the rain.
Under the bridge's
barrier I stood.
Dry as cotton
before the pull.
I waited
on you.

Doorstep

The empty pull
of disappointment,
children's balloon popped,
farewell to kite escaping.

How lost in the well
or random traffic accident
has left me at the doorstep,
hesitating.

Come Home

The walk wasn't it.
It was the road.
Like honey to bees
I took to it 'til the sun
left shining in turn
for winter.
Vines without roses,
trees leafless and frail.

The road firm
with its pleading
taking me beyond
rushes and glory
'til time came calling,
'Come home, come home.'

Over the years,
I often dreamt of coming.
But after beat living,
they'd find me a stranger.

Self-Portrait

"Disturbingly lovely"
was what she said,
after buying
my self-portrait,
thinking,
"Had I only told her."

Direction

Won't sleep
in any direction
other than his.

I remember,
how dark
his skin was
against mine.

When we shot up,
I'd get so bruised,
he'd try to smooth
it all away.

How we stood at the
soup kitchen—holding
love's hand.

How one
can't undo the fate
of another,
and how one
now stands alone.

My Weary Eyes

Whispering
to the night

I still remember
us

sleeping under
the bridge.

Nights you
blanketed
my weary eyes.

Twelve Years Past

Past the delivery room,
through intensive care
to the Morgue,
where reluctantly
I gave up
her identification.

She was the whore
who lived upstairs,
smoked crack
in our bathroom,
hit us up for food,
told us her name was
Destiny.

But twelve years past,
we were roommates
in a home for girls.
I knew her real name,
and in death,
gave it back to her.

For Once

The chill of frost,
ice in my veins.
My breath,
snow falling with
each word.
Blue lips
losing faith in me.
The cops take me in,
and for once,
I'm not resisting.

Neighbor

The girl downstairs
has dyed red hair
cut in a bob
like a hooker
on Baltimore Street.

All day long,
she stays home,
plays with her man's
two overgrown dogs,
talking to them like babies
in her black bodysuit.

One day, she's Cleopatra;
The next, she is Marilyn Monroe.
Tomorrow, she may be
my ex-girlfriend from high school,
the one who wears that bright red lipstick
smothering her face.

Today, she took out the dogs;
all I did was listen to them yap, yap, yap.
Later, I caught her sitting on my doorstep
like a lost piece of jewelry
waiting to be found.

Glories

All the walking
I've done—
the blisters
and burns
I've endured—
the scars
I've gotten
in battles of will.
All glories
from my days
on the road.
None,
I would have
taken back.

A Day Long on Sun

Have you remembered
the days short of rain
long on sun?
By the railroad tracks
under cloudy skies,
two of us became victims
as only I walked away.

Here, by the long building,
we used to sit.
Your cigarette chain-smoking,
my caffeinated cola drink.
Talking 'bout the 'good ole days'
while canvassing the wired fence;
joking in the medicine line
who got the most pills.
You always won
and giggled in pride.
I managed a smile
to soften the blow,
as years later,
I can still hear the trains
trying to screech to a halt.

While driving this morning,
I heard a sheepish giggle;
pulled over to the shoulder,
my face to the sky.
The clouds had all dissipated,
exposing a day long on sun.

Under a Bridge

When the rain
beats down,
temperature drops,
and the only cover
is under a bridge,
it is there that you may
find me.
"Everyone's welcome here."

Outtakes

Stephanie Hiteshew

The Gods

I, Confucius, Me: Hemingway, You:
Homer, we, as you know us—
have found spinning mischief
is like a pinwheel on a windy day.
Here, as in now,
we sit perched atop our chairs, pipe in hand,
blowing dreams away
scattering trash in New York City—
One of many Poets unappreciated by the Man
responds with a sharp tongue—snapping like a whip,
burning flesh to leave you scarred by our history.

Other Half

I swallow sand
become half-desert
dunes under a brutal sky.
Camels horseback riders
cross—
Half of me
wants to take it back.
Water splashes in the blue.
I spit sand and burst
into my other half.
The ocean waves
tumble to the shore.

The Poet

poetry by

B.Z. Niditch

The Poet

B. Z. Niditch

Poet

no cold eyes
may follow
the poet
who waits alone
in hours hidden
from doom to paradise
not expecting
to hear
twilight voices
or change the pain
you only shadow and shatter
the illegible night
caught in every stranger's wound
in the house of friends.

Two in July

Under the wayward gale
the sea shudders
and washes up
the green-blue
breaking my lover's sleep.

If only the lightning
over two survivors
would pass unnoticed
by the summer beachcomber
who, too, wanders
waiting for the gust.

That four-letter word
on the poster bed
angelically dark
on your rose chest.
The Sun surmises
lust striking tumults
where two dusty fringes
watch inaudible stars.

This is a frail morning
by lampstand hours
to offer gifts of petrel.
I remove the shades
feeling echoless
before the frescoes, gardens
dresses, matches
on our sleepless stone.

Moving

It was quiet?
The furniture no longer speaks?
Solitude has fused
your tiny rooms,
the naked fatigue
of a mortal space
between blond teak tables,
evening of something new,
sunlight dissolves
the kitchen,
you want to embrace
the sky.

The Unthinkable

your absent gaze
in the tiny snapshot
about faces
who you were
in a former life
in a deserted time
concealed among caves
and white stones,
the luminous border
cannot even hide you
from yourself.

B. Z. NIDITCH

At Long Island (July 2001)

Thunder scrutinizes the sea
with a dangerous Venus
bent back,
what a paint job
over the cloudless heaven,
fine lines streak,
makes the dawn jealous,
dusk aches and growls
when we want to talk
about art.

Crane's Beach

You put on your 6 a.m. lotion
your round eyes
surfing the cove
on the beach
forgetting your sneakers
in the white sand dunes
wishing for boundless breakers
Poseidon's face
and in the seascape
denim shirt removed
and back twisting
with the rough drafts
of verse in my head
knowing forbidden words
will engage
the incoming tide.

Doom!

Your teacher
calls out an accidental name
but not to you
solitary laughter
from the classless room
of honor-roll monsters
level-headed losers
and popular science playboys.

The name
makes someone pale
she imagines all her years
are in this one moment
she may not look
in the light like you
an accent may be unfamiliar
her language idioms
reversed in disbelief
but doom has settled in
even over her bookish world.

Fall River

Dusk predominates
the loudspeakers by the sea
whiskered poker sharks play
on the copper sand
by the gray wide sails.

Wishing to be a child outdoors
and yet with one sighing wave
to find a green bottle-glass
of some message far gone
bobbing to read any sign.

Now, the night-long wind watcher
takes in its shapeless travel
this absent-minded hour
with the eddies' wordless voice
of the ocean passing roar.

Toward the red moon's darkness
two adolescents weave unwittingly
half-deaf from high tide
like disappearing nymphs
watering your own carved initials.

Past

You lean out of a window
any time
to hear cicadas or sparrows
you are not sorry
on this fall night
the French bread tasted better
and the chocolate pudding
from the warm saucepan
reminded you of childhood
wishing for a slice
of half moons
even though a setting
on the small oak table
always makes you sad.

Online

Logging on wishes
for communicating
what shatters each curiosity
even the mute spider
driven on the wall
has solitude
in wavelengths
warming up the life
of a remote
feeling the exile
wishing to find
a harmonious voice.

B. Z. NIDITCH

Mother Love

Within eighteen seconds
once sleepily speechless
you swear in Italian
at your twin adolescents
about laundry,
luggage and language.

Your tongue
reaches to the house next door
where the sprinkler is turned on
in ecological green violation.

Your daughter overturns
a bathtub Mary
by the neighbor's shrubs
the boy lets a nest loose
and you curse
at your hornet sting.

September 11

They bring on blue skies
on a goatlike city
with an embraced circle
of ice burning terror
on air strata of planes

We look up
from a cherished sunshine
at the sulphureous noise
from September dawn
with a terrible silence

In a mottled deafness
our spirit exploding
at chlorinated reflections
our eyes want to close
at the twin towers burning

Our day is toxic
at the ash faces
wanting to paint the heavens
a different design and form
our bones are still wounded.

Ellis Island

On wavering seas
you streamed
past the authorities
they give you a name
a new T-shirt

No nervousness
in the sunrise
with an emotion
victorious and bigger
than the steps of a slave

A roll call
in the available words
you understand
in the dismal room
through the glass

That short moment
brings back everything else
classic escape
taking this patch
of earth for your own.

Newport
(July 2002)

Even for you
it is odd
to be alone
finding your way
in the budding groves
locating that amulet
hidden in the abandoned field
near the open sea
trying to listen
for the waves to crash
thinking slowly
by the woods' caress
in sea-going temptation
what wonder, stillness, alchemy
burns in and leaps
from unspoken words.

Hampton Beach

With new 9 a.m. binoculars
you survey the cliff dwellers
huge beef embracing
bruised motorcycles
heated leather and tattoos
near the turnpike
where two nymphs dance
to James Brown
in the tumbleweed
giggling with eagerness
will pass a half hour
with perfumed surf
stinging their nostrils
waves curled
in a panic attack
and big-eyed Joe
the eternal lifeguard
knowing he's being watched
removes his Roman shirt
and flips through a road map
for the shy tourists
who deposit towels, lotion and laughter
in Apollo's path.

Separation

you wanted
no self-reproach
to be singleminded
with nameless wishes
finding yourself sunglassed
in a less than congenial home
listening to a frozen dawn
improvisational jazz
children's voices
having rode abandoned
your painful drawings
and maroon bicycle
with a deep silence
of an insomniac world
every invisible night.

Ides of March

spring opens
its asphodel sun
on a sleepwalking river
you snatch
a horizon of hyacinths
by the reeds
for the shy children
next door
March blinded by snow
begging you for answers
from a sky admitting
only a dove-blue dawn
on practical grounds.

Being Thirteen

Outside, it's March
in her ridiculous slippers
you want to tap dance
on black-iced floorboards
and put on that Spanish shawl
Nana sent you
wishing for abandoned fields
feeling immortal
wanting to play horseshoes
but the motionless snow
has not withdrawn
in any clandestine way
you linger by the mirror
demanding time to stop.

On Atlantic Ave.

winter is unyielding
snow falls counterpoint
under gray city walls
the ocean drowns itself
waves wash goodbye
you imagine
a love-bottled letter
on the abandoned beach
where drifts were highest
on dunes, all thoughts
are frozen.

Tales

You want to be
like Rapunzel
climbing ragged vines
or like the first people
crawling in caves
in ancient worlds
making declarations
on white sand
sailing like a slave
on a trading ship
with Ulysses' exiled gestures
by the sea islands
not wanting to imagine
your espoused disaster.

Tar Bar
(New Orleans, March 1988)

Hearing an old Bird chorus
with a low chord
coiled around the bar
bored with the same stories
disdaining the scene
except at dawn
in the densest light,
with the trenchcoat tyrant
in mastering arguments
for your golden sisters
in the breaking riff
with his worn-out talk
and won't accept rejection
jerks against you
with mad regret
like a hurricane
of French fire
you walk away
coolly in the midst of rain.

Recognition

Beneath paintings
that drew
you back to childhood
and the rain's laughter
of grape-shot skies
remembering how they took
your neighbor away
and his portraits
you can't even murmur
a furtive verse
but your lips move
admitting who you are.

B. Z. Niditch

January 1st

The day snow swirls
you also emerge
from a white comforter
your disappearing silence
hidden in a luminous skyline
your life is muffled
in a thousand scarves
chasing bizarre torments
in the unconscious Monday dawn.

Being Fourteen

you compose
resolutions
on the sky's skin
from a radiant sunset
with moonlight dusk
all around your space
you live in delirium
of being fourteen
no worried birthday look
assigning names
to trucks, cut-outs and dolls
wishing to explore
any universe
kept secret.

Brother and Sister

Your child
in dark clothes
hides in abstract paintings
in unexpected disguises
in long-past myths

with other worlds
in mind
from treetops
he stares out
with an absent gaze
hearing his sister
playing the oboe
in the pale air

from veiled light
in the empty August
the dawn sky
makes audible
unrevealed tongues
eclipses faces
through furtive games
of fiery consent.

Adolescence

your early April
hears the city bells
in resting places
by the incense of the moon
singing of reluctant nightshade
in the clear blue air

by a barbed library
on a hidden piano bench
you listen for the unknown
clasping onto your diary
in your short-sleeved yesterday
repeating musical notes
to taste your age
wishing to be at a café
to finger mark a love poem
or to dance forever.

Hiroshima, Mon Amour

You put away
old prints
war toys
and scarred photographs
imagining patches
of quiet grass
surrender blood and bones
only the wind
can hear us
in a handful of urns' ashes
even the strawberries
do not taste the same.

Creativity

Night shadows
keep you awake
like embers in oneness
ideas like ashes
on brown branches
float before your eyes
in the warm air
near the firefly dawn,
lost in silence
the sun observes a day
in the motionless dawn
the light, too, is fleeting
in an abandoned world
giving solitude its morning
and a far-ranging butterfly
in a rare orange repose
casts its dazzling echo
in a page of language.

Outtakes

B. Z. Niditch

1944

You expected the future
to be outlined
in skywriting
but who knew the ridge
of mountain clouds
the soggy days
awaiting liberation.

We can only walk
on tiny pebbles
by the sand dunes
when an earthworm loosens
itself and buries all memory
by the seashore
and shadows trail us
shattering even our freedom.

Wanted!

So you want
to be a soldier
it's better to be mute
when putting on
your uniform.

So you want
to be a beggar
it's better to dream
beside the grave diggers
than ask for help.

So you want
to be a poet
it's better to be
a soldier or beggar
than surprised by words,
unredeemed by life.

At Thirteen

"You always
return to dreams
of youth,"
the old fortune teller
with tattooed palms
tells me.
"Life after childhood
is a nightmare.
You need a lucky number."
I tell him my age
and he says, "Amen,"
and tells me
about Nirvana,
murmuring
about the future.
A gold button
from his topcoat
falls to the ground:
"It's not real.
Nothing is,
only dreams."
He tells me
how he made money
on Wall Street,
and lost it
in the Depression days;
how he joined
the Army to fight fascists,
but was captured
(they played roulette
on his bare chest).
I stuck to "thirteen,"
but afterward
it never brought me luck.

At Fourteen

Consider civilization;
it's advancing,
they tell us;
progress is around
the corner
like love
is next door;
then why is war
just proclaimed
and judges still delay
justice
always till innocence dies,
and why is the miner
beaten in the hallway
and a beggar lies
near the train station;
perhaps it's what
I want to say
that is shut up
between motherland
and fatherland
where some ancient rule
prevails
from left, right, and wrong;
"yet with a smooth stroke
of a young hand
life feels better";
the unabashed sailor
told you to join
the mime company,
but you had to speak
not just pantomime.

About the Author

B. Z. Niditch was born in 1943, a war-child violin prodigy who came of age in the era of Beat and Post-Beat poets, and claims Marcel Proust as his favorite author. He is a poet, playwright, fiction writer, teacher, and aphorist, as well as the founder and artistic director of The Original Theatre in Boston, which has presented original, experimental plays on contemporary social and political themes since 1990. His work has been widely published in journals and magazines throughout the world for decades, including *Columbia: A Journal of Literature and Art*, *The Literary Review*, *Denver Quarterly*, *Hawaii Review*, *Le Guépard* (France), *Kadmos* (France), *Jejune* (Czech Republic), *Leopold Bloom* (Hungary), *Antioch Review*, and *Prairie Schooner*, among other outlets. He lives in Brookline, Massachusetts, and has published numerous chapbooks with small presses, including *Captive Cities*, *Lorca at Seville*, *Fugitive Poet*, *Terezin*, *Boston Fall*, *Childhood*, *Freedom Trail*, and *Everything, Everywhere*, as well as a collection of his aphorisms, *Dictionary of the 21st Century*.

Colophon

The edition you are holding is the First Print Edition of this complete anthology publication. It comprises four previous individual chapbooks originally published without ISBNs, spanning from 2002 to 2010, with single outtake pieces from various other projects spanning from 2008 to 2013. The included chapbooks, now in paperback for the first time, are: *Taxi Cab Poet Confessions: A Small-Press Tribute to Dave Church (1947-2008)* by 22 authors (March 2009), *Billy & Cindy* by Stephanie Hiteshew & Dave Church (October 2009), *Under a Bridge* by Stephanie Hiteshew (November 2010), and *The Poet* by B. Z. Niditch (July 2002).

The cover title font and interior titles are set in Old Newspaper Types, created by Manfred Klein. The alternative non-serif cover font, headers, footers, and captions are set in Avenir Book, created by Adrian Frutiger. The back cover Alternating Current Press logo font is set in Portmanteau, created by JLH Fonts. All other fonts are set in Marion, created by Ray Larabie. All fonts are used with permission; all rights reserved.

The cover was designed by Leah Angstman. The chick watercolor was created by Prawny. The mouse watercolor was created by L. Moonlight. The beetle watercolor was created by MyStocks. The Alternating Current lightbulb logo was created by Leah Angstman, ©2006, 2021 Alternating Current. The Violet Ray logo was created by Leah Angstman, ©2020, 2021 Alternating Current. The cover for *Taxi Cab Poet Confessions* was drawn and painted by Henry Denander, and designed by Leah Angstman. The covers for *Billy & Cindy*, *Under a Bridge*, and *The Poet* were drawn, painted, and designed by Leah Angstman. The photograph of B. Z. Niditch was supplied by the author. All images are used with permission; all rights reserved.

The editors wish to thank the font and graphic creators for allowing legal use of their work.

OTHER WORKS FROM
Alternating Current Press

All of these books (and more) are available at
Alternating Current's website: press.alternatingcurrentarts.com.

alternatingcurrentarts.com